Also by Ellis Sharp

Novels

The Dump
Unbelievable Things
Walthamstow Central
Intolerable Tongues
To Wetumpka
Lamees Najim
The Orwell Girl
Neglected Writer
What Vronsky Did Next
Twenty-Twenty
Alice in Venice
Full English
The Riddle
Month of the Drowned Dog
Pig Tale

Short Fiction

The Aleppo Button
Lenin's Trousers
(with Mac Daly) *Engels on Video*
To Wanstonia
Driving My Baby Back Home
Aria Fritta
Quin Again and other stories
Dead Iraqis: Selected Short Stories

Non-Fiction

Sharply Critical

ELLIS SHARP

CONCRETE IMPRESSIONS

Zoilus Press

A Zoilus Press paperback
First published in Great Britain by Zoilus Press in 2023

A CIP catalogue record for this book is available from the British Library.

ISBN 9781838489892

Cover design by The Ever-Shifting Subject

Typeset by Electrograd

ZOILUS PRESS
York, England

Contents

Alles sag' ich euch ja, weil ich ein Nichts eucht gesagt.

MARX

Part One:
Screaming

11.43am The Infinity Pool

The scream rips apart the bright hot day.

For a second she thinks it's a gull, off course, too far inland, lost, uttering a plaintive piercing plangent protest, until this harsh sharp sound's continuance encourages a brisk reassessment, a sudden troubling recognition that this is no bird's utterance, no animal's harshly emptied lungs, but human in origin, the cry of a man (and not just any man!), a rich urgent thickening cry which curdles inside the soft summery air, its pitch deepening muddily as it diminishes, then thins and stops, only at once to start again.

She, his wife, is at this moment naked – pleasantly adrift on her lilo. Nothing ripples the surface of the infinity pool. It's as still as a frozen fjord, motionless as a laptop screen, flat as the prose of this week's best-selling fiction in *The Times* top ten.

Delphine's eyes are closed. She basks in the warmth like a snug cat. Beneath her eyelids the world is pink, as if seen through a translucent Quality Street wrapper, the strawberry flavour one – a wrapper, along with its colourful companions, to be brutally phased out in the year 2022, making the reference baffling to later generations, like 'mobled queen' in *Hamlet*. As that timeless enchanting unforgettable Echo & The Bunnymen song puts it, nothin' ever lasts forever.

The light from the floating ball of hot plasma 149,598 million kilometres above her has taken eight minutes and twenty seconds to arrive at her breasts, her thighs, her chiselled cheeks.

The hair in her richly abundant pubic region feels soothingly warm and crisp.

She smiles.

In the early days of their love Mick, avidly leaning forwards, nose tilted, fully engaged, had frequently complimented her on her florescence.

She frowns.

The younger generation, bafflingly, scrape off this wondrous thicket of knotty mystery, preferring to revert to an earlier, infantile state. Do they miss their potties and the simple life?

Erasure is a British and American fad.[1] French women are much more in tune with their reeking, hairy, dripping animal selves. *Oui*, she thinks. Hot-blooded mammals have so much more fun than reptiles. Rewilding is better than filling a brown empty field with pigs. Suzanna Hamilton in *Nineteen Eighty-Four* will be remembered long after Ava Verne in *A Thought of Ecstasy* is forgotten.[2]

Somewhere nearby a bumblebee passes, making a noise like a distant outboard motor.[3] In the copse adjacent to the great house a collar dove softly coo-coos. Everything is as quiescent and soothingly soporific as you would expect from a slightly remote part of rural England on a gorgeous sunny day. It is calm, it is placid, it is serene, it is peaceful. If she opens her eyes she knows she will probably see a butterfly flutter past – their estate has whole colonies of blue and amber ones. She can never remember their names, unlike Mick, who is punctilious about detail, though not in the Nabokov league.

Butterflies. Yes, that is what she is thinking about, in a lazy, unfocused, casual manner. What was that novel she had read years earlier, in which a woman – she would die violently at the day's end, was that what happened? – walks through a

[1] 'Erasure is a British and American fad.' Generalisations, although pleasurable for readers of limited intelligence and education, whose lives yawn with lack of direction, are deplorable, as here, because almost always false. Anyone intimately acquainted with progressive British lesbians knows how much they value body hair, both as an identity statement and for sensual reasons which it is not necessary to dip into.

[2] *A Thought of Ecstasy*. Whatever its limitations it does contain some memorable dialogue. The protagonist, Frank, says: 'I'm Frank. I am a character in the book. No, not a character. I am Frank.'

[3] 'Like a distant outboard motor.' Unpardonably vague but from the context the reference is almost certain to be the type of outboard motor seen in *I Spit on Your Grave,* released the year Mick Owen celebrated his thirtieth birthday. He once said to me, 'The original movie is far better than the re-make. No, forget I said that. Please delete that remark. I don't want *that* appearing in my biography! Best not to mention the film at all.' (S. Q.)

cloud of butterflies? A hurricane of giant butterflies approaching the woman's harbour-bound ship, invading it, filling it with fountains of multicoloured stationery. Butterflies which remain with this woman in memory as she stands beside the taxi which has brought her to a square with an empty bandstand and an equestrian statue. Is this square in London? Leningrad? Somewhere in Austria?[4]

Delphine has reached the age where her memories, like *Hamlet*,[5] at times require footnotes and explication.

The butterflies zigzag overhead.

The butterflies vanish astern.

The scream rips apart the bright hot day.

Strangely, at the very moment it occurs, this piercing terrible scream, a cloud obscures the sun. She feels a sudden chill.

It is as if some force greater than any yet known is aware of the awful, dreadful thing which has happened. When monarchs died exactly same thing was evident. Distraught clouds boiled up to honour what was gone, shaping themselves into astonishingly lifelike images of the deceased. And – to take another instance – when the dark, dank, clinging soil beneath the paltry tarmac skin of the car park's surface was gently removed, exposing almost a full set of the bones of Richard III, the sky above Leicester thundered a royal salute while lightning crackled the dead king's delight at the knowledge that he would shortly be upgraded to infinitely superior accommodation.

That mysterious force is also at work where great writers are concerned. When the documentary film makers who followed

4 'What was that novel?' Its title will not require identification to anyone with a rudimentary knowledge of important twentieth-century fiction. The butterflies are of course to be found fluttering around at the beginning of the book's second chapter.

5 'her memories, like *Hamlet*': Of all the liminal devices which nudge the reader towards a greater understanding of the text surely there is none sweeter, none possessed of more illocutionary force, than the footnote. (F. D.)

W. G. Sebald's circuitous route from Norwich to the environs of Bungay let off a firework at the site of his cruel and premature death on the A146 the drifting smoke, astonishingly, shaped itself into the unmistakeable likeness of the author's melancholy face and drooping moustache. They captured it on film. There was no space for doubt.

There are more things in heaven and earth, Horatio...

Delphine takes a deep breath and swings into action. She plunges both hands into the warm water to make paddles. A swift, backward-facing motion and she sends the lilo jerking towards the steel ladder at the pool's edge. Beyond it, on a tiled patio, her white towelling robe is slung over a chair beside the metal outdoor table.

Now she takes hold of the ladder and hauls herself out. Grabbing the robe she throws it on, hurriedly ties the belt and slips on her elegant Dolce & Gabbana sandals.

Then she begins to run.

Breaking News. A commanding, solemn voice and a grave expression: 'The death has been announced...'

For a moment viewers thought the monarch had died. The BBC's male newscasters had put on their black suits and black ties. They were all fans. So, too, were the women. Black skirts; a black blouse over a smart grey jersey shirt. The careful re-arrangement of muscles to produce that serious face you reserve for telling the nation that the monarch was indisposed, that the little prince had toothache, that the rescue effort to save Wanky The Whale, beached and breathless and floppy on Chesil Bank, had sadly, heart-breakingly failed.

'...of a man regarded as the greatest writer of his generation and of our age.'

So, not the monarch.

Dead.

Mick Owen was dead.

The news went viral on Twitter. Not since David Bowie had such a death touched the entire planet.

Abroad, his death was most keenly felt in Germany, where his novels were every bit as popular as those of Rosamunde Pilcher. After that, his biggest fan base was in the United States. The serial killer Barack Obama issued a statement mourning the passing of the greatest non-American writer of the age. The elderly Laura Bush (whose kill total was a paltry one) produced condolences and the memory of a very special afternoon with Mick in London.

In his homeland, Great Britain, he was a giant.

Tomorrow the news of his death and his face would be on the front page of every national newspaper, except the *Daily Star*, whose readers were not great readers and whose editor shrewdly chose a far more compelling story: GIANT RAT EATS MUM'S SEX TOY.

The Guardian was particularly stricken. On the morrow there was a major news feature and an editorial. The obituary occupied two entire pages (though admittedly the paper had been a little anorexic of late, its size shrinking in biannual spasms along with its circulation – down from four million copies a day to just under 100,000). On the following Saturday there was a special commemorative issue – a sprinkling of Mick's old columns for the paper, tributes from fellow writers, old interviews. Later all this, together with all his old columns, would be published as a slender paperback. The *TLS* did the same.

The British Prime Minister (who had graduated from J. K. Rowling to the more adult work of Lee Child) instructed the Culture Minister to come up with something. Since the Culture Minister did not read novels the task was delegated to a subordinate who happily cut and pasted what online material was available in the *Telegraph* archive. Mick Owen, the newspaper had informed its readers just three years earlier, was the eighth most influential figure in British culture, just after Eddie Redmayne at 7 and Eddie Izzard at 6.

But in California there was one man who, though profoundly shaken by the news, did not mourn – at least, not as others mourned. *Totally gutted*, he tweeted, since that was what was expected. In this he was not alone. Social media was a tsunami of emojis. Sad face, weeping face, frowning face, hands-raised-in-horror face. The gutted were in the majority, like fish on a fishmonger's slab. However, an independent-minded minority of the keyboard fraternity went for a studied solemnity. Mick Owen RIP. Dreadful news. Awful news. Shocking news. Praying. Heartbroken.

But though ostensibly eviscerated, Sam Quiggly, in a dark, greasy, secret chamber of his loudly thumping heart felt a stab of ecstasy, a coke-like rush of acute pleasure, a wild rollercoaster whirl of delight and glorious anticipation. These feelings rushed upward into his head. If your mind can have an orgasm then his was having one.

Hallelujah!

Jesus H. Christ!

Yes! Oh yes! Yes!

A wall had fallen. A barrier had been breached. A bright and shining space had opened up.

Sam Quiggly was the freshly deceased's official biographer. He had been working on his *magnum opus* for many, many years. His co-operative subject had insisted on only one condition: that the book not be published until after his death. When Sam had started on his great project he'd happily agreed to this stipulation. There was no hurry and there was much to do. A great deal to do. Back then, Mick Owen was only halfway through his career. But as the years passed Sam felt a growing resentment. In that secret chamber a cold, bitter, exasperated voice could sometimes be heard shrieking: *when is the bastard going to die?*[6]

[6] '*when is the bastard going to die?*': A common sentiment among biographers and memoirists of living novelists. Adverting to the United Kingdom's notoriously unjust libel laws, EU privacy laws and the judiciary's enthusiasm for granting super-injunctions favouring libidinous billionaire bullies, Suleika Dawson reflected that her account of her affair with John le Carré 'would probably have to wait until he was dead'. She added bitterly that at one time it looked as if he was going to live to be 110. Happily, the novelist expired a good twenty-one years earlier, permitting Ms Dawson's delightfully racy

Mick Owen's sixty-fifth birthday had arrived and passed and he seemed physically little changed from the rising literary star of four decades earlier. He was still lean, fit, radiantly healthy. He'd had a tennis court built in the grounds of Kipling Manor and played several times a week with his personal trainer. He cycled and walked daily. He swam. He had never suffered from any serious illness. This could not be said of his biographer. At the age of forty-nine poor Sam Quiggly had required a heart by-pass operation. Three years later he'd had a brush with cancer, necessitating the removal of a small portion of his nose. As his draft biography had grown (165,000 words and then 220,000 and then 305,000 – and now somewhat more than that), so, too, had Sam's waist. He yearned for those younger, skinnier days when he was a mere thirteen stones in weight, with a 36-inch waist. Nowadays his blood pressure was far too high, his complexion unevenly florid. His penis, like the neurotic girlfriend who had blighted his mid-twenties, had developed a distressing tendency to shed tears without warning. He now had to wear a gentleman's pad in his underwear to avoid signalling with fresh, dark, pomegranate-sized stains in the vicinity of his crotch his tragically uncontrollable condition.

Plus he drank too much. He really, really wanted to cut back but every day by 4pm reality grew tired and grey and seemed to require a shot of liquid fire to warm it up and give it colour. Quiggly did his best work between 11pm and 2am, lubricated by a bottle and a half of red wine. He told himself this was moderation in action. Patrick Hamilton, he knew, had consumed a bottle of spirits a day, minimum. As for Charles Jackson and Malcolm Lowry...

And now that unspoken long-yearned-for day had come. He could at long last wrap the goddam book up. *Mick Owen: The Life* had become a nightmare and he'd be glad to have done with it. The windmills of Quiggly's mind began to accelerate

account of their time together to be published. See *The Secret Heart: John le Carré, an Intimate Memoir* (2022).

and spin in blurred circles. He realised that the sound of distant drumming was merely the fingers of his hand, restless for his laptop's keyboard. The biography could be brought forward now, at speed. He would wrap it up with the funeral. He knew Delphine did not like him but she could not deny him that. As a precaution he had confirmed his attendance in advance with Mick many years ago. He had it in writing, signed. And once that was done, that was pretty much it. His publishers, normally sluggish about publication, would see to it that the book was rushed out, to profit from the inevitable surge of interest in the now dead novelist. There would be the book launch and a round of interviews. These would be fun. He would encounter attractive women, some of them considerably younger than he was. One or two of them might be prevailed upon to come to his hotel room...

Sam chuckled. It was not yet 4pm but he saw no reason why he should not indulge in a liquid celebration. Death is always a fabulous career move for any writer (though this sales phenomenon is even more noticeable in the world of popular music). It helped if the concrete circumstances of the passage into immortality were sexy. Nabokov drifting quietly off in a hospital room in Lausanne was dull, dull, dull. Whereas Sylvia Plath was a smart cookie. No one had ever understood *marketing* and the importance of a *brand* better than her. That's what most writers failed to grasp. If you seriously want to make it big you need a USP. Keats checking out at twenty-five was one hell of smart move. An early death, blood and pain, an eloquent last speech, a fan museum located right next to the Spanish Steps – the guy knew what jangled people's bells and he sure understood the importance of being convenient for tourists.

Still grinning, Sam Quiggly looked out at the great belt of smoke and dust which had begun to drift across San Francisco Bay. Soon an orange haze began to dissolve and mask the outlines of things. California was burning again but, heck, he didn't care! The planet might be fucked but he had a book coming out. Nothing compared to that.

11.44am The Lawn

Delphine runs fast across the lush green lawn towards the house.

Cloud still obscures the sun. A grey sheet, unrolling across the blue sky. Nimbostratus. There will be rain later.

The screaming continues. Her directional hearing is acute and she knows exactly where it is coming from. Up there in the tower. Mick's writing room.

And it is Mick who is screaming. He sounds in extreme distress. He needs urgent assistance.

She sprints towards the house, breathing heavily. The belt falls away and her robe opens like the white wings of a gigantic butterfly. With a grunt of irritation she raises both hands and flicks the garment from her shoulders. The robe drops away behind her.

She runs on, nude.

They had bought the house and its estate ten years earlier. Driving around Suffolk on holiday they'd seen the FOR SALE sign by the entrance on a quiet country lane not far from Yoxford. Mick steered the car off the road and they passed between a pair of crumbling lichen-dappled stone pillars topped by stone pineapples. A sign said IPLING MANOR – PRIVATE.

Ipling?

Later, they discovered that the first letter was missing. Mick was excited, sensing a connection with the author of *The Jungle Book* and *Kim*. The first English language writer to be awarded the Nobel Prize in Literature (as it should really be called)! *In consideration of the power of observation, originality of imagination, virility of ideas and remarkable talent for narration that characterize the creations of this world-famous author*. Which, when you thought about it, sounded like a very precise description of his own current achievement in fiction, Mick reflected. No one's ideas were surely as virile as his – at least not where the contemporary novel was concerned...

Alas, Wikipedia failed to supply any hint of an association between Rudyard Kipling and Suffolk. Where writing was concerned Suffolk yielded only *The Rubáyáit of Omar Khayyam*, George Orwell and *The Rings of Saturn*, plus a couple of popular women crime writers. But that was then and this was now. Now fate decreed forsooth that the name Mick Owen would be added to this East Anglian list – a glittering star destined to long outshine those other pale and minor moons.

Moving along the twisting, bumpy, weed-lined drive in the twin-exhaust blood-red Merc they at last arrived at the house. It was bigger than any property they'd ever owned – eight rooms wide at the front, three storeys high, with dormers in the roof and a clock tower which lacked a clock. Plus long wings folded away at the sides, tidy as a pterodactyl's.

Lots of space for Mick's books.

The place was uninhabited. You could see at a glance that the rooms were bare. The ivy-darkened windows and the unkempt porch gave the house a faintly sinister aspect. Anarchic surges of purple-tinted Virginia creeper lapped the walls.

It was like something from a fairy tale. A house under a strange enchantment; a house of ghosts. You might almost expect to meet Miss Havisham upstairs, in a dark room at the back, muttering to herself, white-haired and worn and in her bridal dress. (Be sure to take a fire extinguisher with you.)

Mick walked up the diamond-patterned tiled steps which led to the front door. Brushing past a surge of thistles he disturbed a beetle, which scampered in fear along the third step and vanished abruptly into a crack.

Mick thumped the door hard with the brass knocker, which was fashioned in the shape of what might almost have been supposed to resemble a tablet of soap. The sound echoed inside the house and faded. Several leaf-like flakes of paint floated away from the door panels in response to the brief seismic activity.

He shrugged; jitterbugged; tugged at his collar; then lugged his flesh and his complex sensibility back to Delphine. Hand-in-hand, like ardent lovers at the start of a passionate romance, they went off to explore the grounds.

The lawn at the rear was knee-high in grass. They trudged across it and paused at the start of a track that led off into woodland. Ignoring his hero Bob Dylan's advice, Mick looked back. He gasped (which is good for the lungs) and cried, 'Look!'

He saw now that the clock tower which was not a clock tower was a more substantial structure than he'd at first appreciated. It resembled an enclosed viewing platform – a square wood-panelled room with oval windows and a pointed roof. Mick sensed that it would make an amazing place in which to write. It was very private, not overlooked, and it must surely be full of natural light. Plus the views were surely spectacular from up there. Yes, it was the perfect creative den for a novelist who favoured omniscience and psychological realism. God always needed to be higher than everyone else, in order to know everything that's going on below. *Everything*. (One of his first purchases as a best-selling writer had been a pair of very expensive Zeiss Victory binoculars.)

They moved on, his pulse ticking a little faster now.

The overgrown track was a green tunnel which led through over-arching thick-bellied yews to emerge at the kidney-shaped lake. This, too, looked neglected. A ramshackle boat shed with missing panels looked out over a wooden pier in a similarly parlous state. Beside the pier a submerged, rotting rowing boat protruded from the reed-infested muddy water.

They walked round the lake.

A creamy emerald scum had accumulated at the western end, where a choked-up sluice gate was just visible under an accumulation of branches and a brown sludge of malodorous vegetable matter. Nearby, lilies of the valley grew in profusion. Their sweet perfume seemed to impregnate Mick's clothes. Strangely, the aroma lingered there for weeks.

They returned the next day with the estate agent, who, scenting that his commission might finally materialise, confided that the owners would be happy to knock 80K off the asking price, just to be shot of the place. The property had been on the market for over a year and, though a number of prospective purchasers had viewed it, they had all rejected it on the grounds of the cost of the much-needed renovation work. The house, though structurally sound, suffered from damp and mould, a broken boiler, and ancient electrical wiring that needed ripping out. Its numerous cracked windows with softly decomposing frames were equally in desperate need of replacement. Apart from all that, the entire house needed redecorating. As for the estate, it would necessitate a team of gardeners to clear it, prune it, and replant it. That sluice gate required cleaning out. The boating shed would have to be demolished and replaced, as would the pier. There was a sluggish stream which cried out for dredging and repair work to its fallen banks.

'We'll take it,' Mick said, and the agent beamed, for Christmas Day had come.

The cost of bringing the place up to scratch would be almost equal to the sale price, but so what? By now Mick was a multi-millionaire. And so, once the place was theirs, they rented a house in Walberswick and went off to see their architect and builders to sort out the changes that were needed.

Mick spent some time in the Suffolk Records Office and discovered the history of Kipling Manor. The man behind it was not Rudyard but Russell. This Kipling was a hugely successful manufacturer of soap (hence the door-knocker). His business involved a much reproduced advertisement which at the time had become part of the nation's consciousness. It showed a naked young woman with curly hair and rosy cheeks smiling invitingly as she turned her head sideways to face the viewer from her tin bath. Her legs were bent and the angle of display showed the twin peaks of her raised, parted knees and a pale slice of naked shoulder. It was accompanied by a slightly risqué caption in a large blue copperplate: *Kipling Soap – Nothing Smells Quite as Good as This!*

This particular bloated capitalist in a top hat purchased the forty acres of land in 1897. In those days the site was forest. He had swathes of it cut down, and a lake scooped out, to be filled by a diverted stream. Land nearby was cleared for the construction of a large house. Kipling spelled out to the architect what he wanted: a cross between that architectural wonder of the region, Somerleyton Hall, and the Arts and Crafts style. There was a house on Park Lane, Southwold, which he particularly admired.

'Kipling Manor' was duly built, between January 1900 and November 1903. Mr Kipling moved in the following February. Mick often thought of the soap giant. Sometimes he could almost feel his presence – a big, bearded man standing on the lawn in a velvet smoking jacket, puffing on a cigar as he contemplated the first yellowish streaks of a new day. What would the future bring? His mission to make the working class less smelly was already well on its way to being accomplished (apart from those troublesome legions of grimy slum-dwellers who chose to shun his product). It was a marvellous time to be alive. Everything was so peaceful. That spot of bother in the Transvaal had been sorted out – no thanks to Miss Emily Hobhouse.

The British Empire had gifted a new form of humanitarian organisation to the world: the concentration camp. It was splendidly efficient yet Miss Hobhouse was determined to denigrate it. She made wild, fantastic claims of mass starvation; of typhoid; of sick children; of thousands upon thousands of deaths. (There were agitators who came up with similarly wild allegations about conditions in the Congo Free State, from where Mr Kipling obtained the palm oil for his softest soap.) Miss Hobhouse alleged that people were taken to these camps in trains. Distraught women and children seen in railway sidings in open trucks – starved, rained-on! And worse. It was most unpleasant to read at breakfast of filth-encrusted latrines and unemptied pails.

It was a lot of nonsense, of course. Kitchener himself had assured the nation that there was only one word to describe the condition of the people in the camps: 'happy'. People went there quite voluntarily. There were facilities for lawn tennis. While admittedly there may at times have been discomforts, these were being alleviated.

In truth, Mr Kipling was perturbed by only one item on Miss Hobhouse's lurid inventory of failings: 'no soap'. He sensed a missed export opportunity.

You only had to read *The Times* to know that things were going swimmingly out there. Their man on the spot, Leo Amery, painted a very reassuring picture of the state of things. There was simply nothing at all to get worked up about. You could sit at home and play whist with a clear conscience. As for Miss Hobhouse, the newspapers were united in calling her a 'screamer'. Poor woman. She was forty-one, unmarried. She attracted the adjective 'dumpy'. This loud, troublesome woman had something missing in her life and every red-blooded Englishman (grin, wink) knew what it was.

Mr Kipling exhaled more smoke. Is there a more delicious aroma than smoke from a fat Havana cigar? Only one, unfit to be mentioned in a homely narrative for the bourgeoisie.

Yellow had turned to bronze, bronze to red. Now, abruptly, as the sun began its slow climb, there was gold – a gigantic bar of it, resting on a bed of pure blue. Starlings awoke and began to congregate, over a century in advance of their time, greeting the dawn with their tweets.

Mr Kipling smiled. Despite the Miss Hobhouses of this world it was a fact that the Anglo-Saxon race was spreading progress around the entire planet. The mentally undeveloped ones were falling by the wayside. As Darwin had established, this was nature's way. The inherent vigour of the white race overcame the lower races. The eradication of savages was inevitable. The Tasmanians had quite simply vanished. The population of the Maori people in New Zealand had halved.

Struggle – Darwin again! – is the very essence of life itself. It ennobles *Homo sapiens*. As the Prime Minister had said in the Albert Hall – it seemed like only yesterday – 'One can roughly divide the nations of the world into the living and the dying.' How very true! The progressive nations had taken control of northern Asia, North America, South America, Africa and Australia. In Southwest Africa the Herero people were commanded to depart from their land so that German companies and German settlers might bring progress to a backward part of Africa. The savages resisted. In October 1904 General Adolf Lebrecht von Trotha ordered their extermination. *Iron severity completed the work of annihilation. The death rattles of the dying resounded in the sublime silence of infinity.* A good name, Adolf. Solidly German.

Yes, a marvellous time for an Edwardian gentleman to be alive...

By the time he had finished his cigar the sun was over the trees and a delicious smell of frying bacon drifted across the lawn. Mr Kipling went indoors to wash his hands with the company's most expensive bar of lavender soap.

After the soap titan's death from an apoplexy in 1910, provoked by strikes at his factories, his only son Archie decided that the house lacked an essential ornament – a tower. This was added to the roof and completed on 15 April 1912. Alas, Archie did not enjoy his tower for very long. The following year he boarded a hot-air balloon, which malfunctioned. His companions jumped free, leaving him alone. He was last seen drifting over the German Ocean, gesticulating furiously, like a novelist reading a bad review.

There were a number of subsequent owners, devoid of narrative interest. Then Mick arrived and the house entered literary history. It was henceforth as distinguished as that refurbished pub on Henley Street or the enlarged house with exquisite Laura Ashley wallpaper at the summit of a steep cobbled hill in dismal Yorkshire. In due course, after the funeral and the publication of Sam Quiggly's masterwork, and the employment of a curator, it would eventually open to the public, just like 48 Doughty Street with its cabinet of cutlery (including the actual knife which the novelist had used to shovel fish down his gullet!), or Dove Cottage, or that property in Chawton with its fascinating display of period embroidery.

Mick, a man of taste, restored Kipling Manor so that from outside it much resembled its original incarnation. Inside, it was entirely transformed, to make a bright, modern habitation fit for a successful writer. The chairs in the Purple Room (used exclusively for eating fruit) were sourced exclusively from an antique dealer in Berlin. The Yellow Room was designed for guests to eat soup made entirely from local vegetables. A professional was brought in for tablescaping, arranging products from Mrs Alice & Talmaris, the by-appointment-only tableware store in Paris. As a delightful postmodern touch Mick kept the old embroidered bell ropes in the bedrooms. The long disconnected clappers in the servants' quarter in the basement added a nice touch to the massive wine cellar. Al Stewart, whom Mick had seen sing at St Andrews Hall in Norwich in 1972, gazed admiringly at the cobwebbed bottles and complimented Mick on his exceptional taste.

Like Jay Gatsby, the novelist had come a long way to this place. Born in 1948 to parents who lived in a post-war prefab on the edge of York, he had long since shed his humble origins. Now he was one of the wealthiest and most famous writers in Britain; now he dined with celebrities from every walk of life.

And now he was screaming.

Now he was in deep distress.

Delphine reaches the large paved area that led to the conservatory. A few scattered drops of chlorinated pool water mark her route, like tell-tale blood deposited by someone in flight, who has been shot.

She knows there are two people in particular who might want to murder Mick Owen. There are many others she can think of who loathe and despise him – there were ancient friendships which had soured, not to mention entire legions of lesser, envious, resentful writers. Even her own father – that insurrectionary reflexive pronoun is surely necessary here, for emphasis – was scathing about the calibre of his work. But Ferdinand, mercifully, no longer visited. He preferred Paris and the charms of whichever deluded young woman had become his latest mistress.

Poor Mick. Social media was a curse. It was a Babel of screeching voices, where the forlorn and the failed each day squirted their little jets of displeasure. But though the internet's stinging smog of commentary hung over the pure, blazing admiration and respect for Mick Owen which shone throughout the corporate media, she very much doubted that a single one of those peevish keyboard warriors really was sufficiently unhappy as to engage in a vicious physical assault.

No.

There were only two people in the world who would be thrilled to see Mick Owen dead and who seemed actually capable of expediting delivery of that particular explosive package.

Delphine runs on, wondering which of the two it might be.

11.45am The Conservatory

His screams continue, rhythmical, as regular as a drum beat.

You cannot help but think of the First Folio's brilliantly economical use of typography in expressing Hamlet's dying groans. O, o, o, o. Upper-case 'O' followed by the same three letters in lower case. Three commas, followed by a full stop. That final punctuation mark which lies in wait for us all.

And what is it that this letter signifies? Three things. The circular shape of Hamlet's mouth as his lips stretch out for his final utterance. The nature of that utterance – a loud groan followed by three quieter groans. Hamlet's life is ebbing at a speed far faster than the motion of any tide. His entire existence is draining away, and his mouth is the end of the waste pipe, the outlet from which it falls. And when it is over, when the last groan's gone, what then? Why, oblivion. Nothing. Zilch. *Zero*.

No, make that four things.

For what else is that letter 'O' than a mirror of the place wherein forsooth this drama was first acted out? The Globe. A world – a universe – contained within a structure like a giant Polo mint, made out of sturdy Tudor timber.

The quickest, most direct route to the grand staircase lies through the conservatory. Delphine wrenches the door open and dashes inside. The accumulated hot air beneath the glass roof is as syrup-thick and clammy as a *Guardian* opinion piece. It is like stepping into a sauna. Her breathing becomes laboured, as if the oxygen in here is somewhat depleted.

Her feet slither on the burning flagstones. Everything seems coated in condensation. She slows her pace. It would not do to fall and fracture one's femur or fibula or fuck with the fascia of one's forearm.

Mick's screams continue but they are deflected and muffled by the surrounding glass panes.

She passes the wickerwork chairs, the wickerwork table, the potted palms, the voodoo plants from East Ruston Old

Vicarage Garden, the bookcase crammed with history books. Orlando Figes, Anthony Beevor, Andrew Roberts, Simon Schama, Max Hastings, Tom Holland, Sathnam Sanghera, Andrew Marr, David Olusoga, Dan Snow, Jeremy Paxman – all the great historians of the age.

Books everywhere. Mick was an addict. No matter how big the houses that he lived in, none was ever big enough for his library. He never disposed of any books to charity shops (Thrift, thrift, Horatio). He kept every one he had ever bought. He was still angry regarding three loans he had made in the course of a lifetime which had never been returned. In 1962 he had let Arthur, a school friend, borrow his paperback copy of William L. Shirer's *The Rise and Fall of the Third Reich.* Arthur's family moved unexpectedly and Mick never saw his book again. In 1973 the poet Ellie Short asked to borrow his Penguin *Crime and Punishment.* She also went off without ever returning it. Three years later, in Africa, he lent his precious hardback first edition of *Conference of the Birds* to Maggie, the wife of a bank manager. He never got it back. That was the last book he ever loaned. He had learned a bitter lesson.

On the lowest shelf, squeezed in next to a set of wrinkled Pelicans, are three books by Norman Cohn: one on the Genesis story, one on witch-hunts, one on revolutionary millenarians.

Was his use of a text by this latter writer comically allusive or simply unconscious when Mick gave the 2007 Wisdom Lecture at Harvard? (One would need to ask God but He currently isn't answering his phone.)

The Lecture created a sensation. In his biography Sam Quiggly devoted seven pages to it. He described it as the key to understanding Mick's work and ethical sense.

'My fellow Americans,' Mick began.

That made his audience sit up. Frowns and whispers. Puzzled faces. What had gotten into him? What was he playing at? Everyone knew Mick Owen was a Brit. He'd been born in Old York in 1948. His passport, once black, was now smaller and plum-coloured, with a microchip and laminated pages. He was British but he was also a proud European. Those white stars on a blue background meant the world to him. But not as much as those fifty other stars which illuminated thirteen adjacent stripes.

Smiling, Mick explained what he meant by his teasing opening sentence. He was, he said, American in everything except his citizenship. 'In spirit I am an American because no one is freer than an American! The creative spirit is nowhere more creative, more boundary-breaking, than in America! The creative spirit burns nowhere more brightly in the world than here!'

A good beginning. How the audience roared their approval! The standing ovation endured for three minutes fifty-seven seconds. A record for any of the Wisdom speakers at that date. Eventually President Zelensky of Ukraine did better – but that was years later.

'Freedom is everywhere in this land,' he continued. 'In what other country in the world is burning the national flag protected by law? Try it and see.' (Laughter; more applause.)

'Free speech guaranteed under the First Amendment to the United States Constitution! Something most societies and cultures around the world can only dream of.'

This led him on to the American novel – the freest, richest, deepest, most innovative narrative form yet to exist. Mick said he wanted to pay a special tribute to the late Saul Bellow. He'd been an inspiration to him from his earliest days as a writer. When he learned of the novelist's death he dropped everything and sat down to re-read *Mr Sammler's Planet*. What a magnificent novel that was!

Here was a blistering satire on 'cancel culture' which was decades ahead of its time! What was more poignant than that awful moment when septuagenarian Artur Sammler attempts to address a large audience of young students about some twentieth-century English writers and intellectuals, including George Orwell? Poor Sammler is shouted down by a student revolutionary. The student has a beard and is wearing jeans. He shouts that Orwell 'was a sick counter-revolutionary'. He tells Sammler he is speaking 'a lot of shit'. He says it is good that Orwell died prematurely. He tells the audience that Sammler is an 'effete old shit' whose testicles have dried-up. 'He can't come.' The heckler has the audience with him.

'But this is America. Land of the free! A democracy! And Bellow summarises what it is to be a citizen of this great nation. He describes how "the charm, the ebullient glamour, the almost unbearable agitation that came from being able to describe oneself as a twentieth-century American was available to all." But with freedom comes self-indulgence, of the kind seen when Sammler is shouted down. And how ironic is that? For Sammler is a Holocaust survivor. Or as Bellow puts it, [7]

[7] 'as Bellow puts it': the liberal novelist purportedly gives the reader two opposing perspectives and allows the reader to decide which is the more persuasive. Or so bourgeois liberal critics would have us believe, though in reality they are simply staring into a mirror and giggling with pleasure and admiration at what they see, which is not the cracks in the glass or the blood soaking the carpet and splattered across the wall. The objections to *Mr Sammler's Planet* are numerous. Much of the book consists of a stream – sewer? – of consciousness, conveyed in clogged and stodgy prose. The scene with the student radical is so lurid and wildly exaggerated as to lack all credibility – but then Bellow is representing in a cartoon form the anxiety of a right-wing author adrift in a modern world he resents and resists. Even though the novel is set in 1970s New York it articulates the paranoia of the timeless *Daily Mail* reader. The police won't come when you want them! Vandals are breaking things and urinating in the street! Students are hairy and dirty and infantile and they don't clean their shoes! Women have lost their grace and femininity and are sexually threatening! What awfulness emanates from 'female generative slime'! Now they aren't just wearing miniskirts – some even flaunt themselves in microskirts! Marriage is being undermined by lax sexual morals and pornography! Black criminals are getting away with it while the police turn a blind eye! (The figure of the absurdly implausible student heckler is matched by that equally implausible and inherently racist cartoon character, the tall, smartly dressed black pickpocket – a threatening individual who terrorises poor Sammler by tracking him down to his home and displaying his penis to him.) But

in this world of chaos and disorder there is one source of stability, bravely holding out against the anarchy of things. Yes (unbelievably, offensively, preposterously), Israel. In New York a Holocaust survivor like Sammler is under perpetual threat. 'In Jerusalem there were more old relatives like Sammler.' One character confides that 'They're making terrific stuff in Israel these days.' We hear of Israeli wine and brandy and silver pens. We hear of the purchase of 'Israel bonds and real estate'. *Real estate!* In two casual words surface the hollow liberal morality which underpins *Mr Sammler's Planet.* The theft of a country – the violent, barbaric dispossession of almost an entire population, one of the fastest and greatest land and property thefts in history – is obliterated from the consciousness of Bellow's puppets, just as it has no existence for their creator. 'I believe I'll go to Jerusalem for a while,' a character casually remarks, expressing the privileges of travel for an American Jew – a privilege denied to those whose real estate was wrenched from them with extreme violence, without compensation. 'I love it there,' chuckles our character. Fast forward to 2023. Palestinians in Jerusalem are subjected to daily violence by settlers, police and a bureaucracy that aims to push them out of the city. Israel's racist soldiers commit massacres and atrocities on a regular basis, while the USA and the UK supply the weaponry, and the EU winks its approval. Because *Mr Sammler's Planet* is a liberal novel there is a character who is anti-Zionist, although he, too, is a puppet – an incarnation of Bellow's shrivelled understanding. The anti-Zionist provocateur argues that 'the modernization Israel was bringing to the Middle East was altogether too rapid for the Arabs'. Yes, in this novel even the anti-Zionists speak the language of Zionism. And the anti-Zionist, like the lefties in a Mick Owen novel, is a shallow, risible figure; he displays a 'sudden passion (soon vanishing) for Arab culture'. Whereas the Zionists are loveable, whimsical people who display delightful idiosyncrasies: 'His one glamorous eccentricity was to fly to Israel on short notice and stroll into the King David Hotel without baggage, his hands in his pockets. That struck him as a sporting thing to do.' It would require a book to unpack the complacency and the moral blankness of Saul Bellow which cushions sentences like those. Even the wars of a belligerent racist settler state – Israel has now bombed no less than seven Arab states – are represented as being defensive. All the stale apologias for Zionist violence are served up in *Mr Sammler's Planet*, sprinkled with cheap

"He was only an old Jew whom they had hacked at, shot at, but missed killing somehow." And who are the inheritors of Nazism? The students. And others. The most chilling figure in the book is surely the black pickpocket, who tracks our hero to his apartment block and exposes himself as a warning. This is perhaps the most terrifying moment in modern fiction.'

Mick cleared his throat. 'Saul Bellow was consumed by the

perfume. No surprise that when Mr Sammler visits Gaza under military occupation he recoils from its women. Whereas New York women torment him with their unrestrained sexuality, Palestinian women are hard and unattractive: 'heavy-boned mannish faces... large noses, the stern mouths projecting over stonelike teeth'. If a Palestinian writer had ever described Jewish women as ugly, with *large noses*, you can be sure this would have been duly noted, magnified throughout the corporate media as a shocking example of enduring Arab anti-Semitism, endlessly recited and repeated down the years, and a storm of protest would have accompanied the award of a Nobel Prize – quickly, Monique, fetch the vomit bucket! – 'for the humane understanding and subtle analysis of contemporary culture that are combined in his work'. Incidentally, apropos that terrifying black pickpocket, the United States has the highest incarceration rate of any nation in the world. Currently some 2 million people – 1/166th of its population – are behind bars. And – just fancy that! – young black men are six times more likely to be imprisoned than their white peers. No surprise that a racist ignoramus and Israel worshipper like Saul Bellow should a few years later provide a testimonial for Joan Peters' fraudulent book *From Time Immemorial* (1984). Not that Bellow was exactly alone in seeking to justify Israeli barbarism in Lebanon in 1982 by trying to revive discredited Zionist myths. Bob Dylan did the same. You will often hear T. S. Eliot accused of anti-Semitism but you are unlikely ever to read about Dylan's vile and disgusting song 'Neighbourhood Bully', which attempts to drown out the great chorus of screams rising from Sabra and Shatila. But that didn't bother the Nobel Prize committee which gave Dylan his bauble and which the multi-millionaire outlaw was happy to accept. (Bob's speech incidentally pays tribute to *Moby-Dick*, one of his favourite books. Evidently the singer never noticed the hyphen in all his readings.) Mick Owen, of course, has on many occasions spoken of his enthusiasm for Dylan's work. But not, one hopes, *Tarantula*.

sense of an ending and the monsters which it can bring to birth. And when we think of the sense of an ending – of its seductions and satisfactions – let us recall Norman Cohn's seminal study of European apocalyptic movements, *The Pursuit of the Millennium.*

'Cohn describes the devastating influence of the scriptural analysis of Joachim of Fiore, a twelfth century Italian monk. Joachim concluded that the Bible held a secret meaning. Decoded, it revealed that history had a pattern. There were three great phases. The first stretched from Adam to Abraham, the second from Elijah to Christ. The third was from St Benedict to the time of Joachim of Fiore. It meant that the apocalypse was about to happen, ushering in the Age of the Spirit.

'The sense of an ending is always with us. It inflames the mob. The mob runs amok. It lusts for a perfect society. Perfection requires the elimination of obstacles to perfection. Often it was the Jews. Sometimes it was women, who made a pact with the Devil and became witches. Frequently it was property owners.

'This terrible passion endured across centuries and cultures. In the mid-seventeenth century The Diggers, led by Gerrard Winstanley, pursued the vision of a world without private property and class distinctions. Another sect, The Ranters, also sought the revolutionary overthrow of existing society.

'There is a chilling account by George Fox, the Quaker, of his experiences in prison in Coventry. There he encountered fellow prisoners who "began to rant, and vapour, and blaspheme, at which my soul was greatly grieved". Fox listened in horror as "They said they were God". But Fox had the edge on them. "I asked them if they knew whether it would rain tomorrow." The response? "They said they could not tell." Fox smiled knowingly. "I told them, God could tell."

'It's a frightening anecdote. As Fox noted, The Ranters were "very rude, and sung, and whistled, and danced". They were not religious. "They called for drink and tobacco, one cried 'all is ours'."

'As Cohn shrewdly notes, from Joachim of Fiore and The Diggers and Ranters there is a clear and obvious line of descent to the Marxian thesis of primitive communism, class society, and a final communism in which the state withers away.

'Today – Cohn again – those fascinated by ideas of apocalypse are the populations of certain technologically backward societies, overpopulated, desperately poor, dislocated and disorientated, as well as politically marginal elements in technologically advanced societies – chiefly young or unemployed workers and a small minority of intellectuals and students. Since 1917 there has been the steady growth of what Cohn calls "phantasies of a final, exterminatory struggle against 'the great ones'; and 'of a perfect world from which self-seeking would be for ever banished'".

'In short, Cohn concludes, the old religious idiom has been replaced by a secular one, and this tends to obscure what would otherwise be obvious. For it is the simple truth that, stripped of their original supernatural sanction, evolutionary millenarianism and mystical anarchism are with us still.'

Mick's pause was of the pregnant sort. He was about to give birth to his incisive and impressive conclusions.

'But where does 1917 and all its horrors – Stalin, the trials, the Gulag archipelago! – come from? In the second instance – Berlin! Let us go back in time to the University of Berlin and the fall of 1836. Had you been there at that time you might have glimpsed a typical fashionably attired student of the age. He has long hair, a pencil-thin moustache, a wispy, tiny beard. He is handsome, romantic, over-emotional. He is still a teenager, yet he has impulsively and furtively become engaged to an aristocratic older woman. He is at this time a student of law, with a solid legal career ahead of him. With due diligence he could become an attorney, with an agreeable house, a pleasant garden, servants. But in Berlin in those first months he shows himself more interested in literature than law. He begins to think of himself as a poet; as a playwright; as a novelist; as a theatre critic. You might think, where's the harm in that? But note what kind of novel our somewhat intense young man endeavours to write. Fortunately, though never completed, it has survived.

'*Skorpion und Felix*. You have never heard of it? Of course you haven't. Do not blame yourselves. Very few people have. Despite the subsequent fame of its author – or should I say *infamy*? – it has never been translated. It is perhaps the most obscure of all the writings of a man whose name is now globally known and who even today is revered by some of the most noxious regimes on earth. In *Mr Sammler's Planet* Saul Bellow brilliantly cuts him down to size as "that furious world-boiler". Yes, professors and doctors, graduates, postgraduates and undergraduates, ladies and gentlemen, the fellow of whom I speak is one *Karl Marx*. Before he became perhaps the planet's most pernicious political propagandist of violent insurrection he attempted to become a novelist.

'Remember, incidentally, that Hitler was an execrable painter and Stalin a mediocre poet. The genocidal mind is strangely – albeit it feebly and flimsily – creative in its earliest incarnations. Beware painting groups dedicated to watercolours and views of yachts in estuaries. Beware Picasso seminars and poetry and reading groups. Beware afternoon lectures on architecture.

'Marx subtitled his novel *Ein humoristischer Roman – A Humorous Novel*. One might observe that if you have to point out to the reader that your novel is a comedy than perhaps the laughter evoked by the text will be of microscopic proportions.' (Laughter; applause.)

Pause.

'I cannot pretend to have read this incomplete narrative. The German language is a monster which I have preferred to flee rather than slay.' (Laughter.) 'However. I have paid sincere attention to the analysis of those who have. Peter Demetz in particular. He describes the narrative as shambolic, incoherent, a complete disaster. Its author, he concludes, was a dilettante. Yet the fact that Marx abandoned it I suppose indicates that in some respects at least he had an acute critical intelligence.' (Laughter.) 'Demetz describes the novel as little more than an inventory of crude jokes, forced literary associations and a chaotic wilderness of puns. I must say I am rather reminded of the work of one of my contemporaries – his name is Sharp and you need not write it down.' (Laughter.) [8] 'Demetz, who, bafflingly for a refugee from Communist Czechoslovakia, was something of an admirer of Marx, sums up *Skorpion und Felix* as "without order, force, or effect".

'Another scholar who has also taken the trouble to read this obscure text[9] describes it as a "clumsy anti-bourgeois satire" full of "sudden deliberate let-downs" and "verbal cartoons". It also "drags in, at every opportunity" allusions to the Bible, Ovid, Johann Joachim Winckelmann, Goethe, Oliver Goldsmith, E. T. A. Hoffmann, Schiller, Shakespeare, Hegel, Heine, Gottfried Wilhelm Leibniz, Christian Wolff, Kant, Wilhelm Traugott Krug, and Ernst Raupach.

'And what was Marx's template for this cacophony of clutter? What was his inspiration? It pains me to say this, but it was an English novelist. That is, if you can call *The Life and Opinions of Tristram Shandy, Gentleman* a novel!

'In short, there is a direct line from the horrors of Stalin, via Marx, to the so-called experimental novel. That Laurence Sterne was an inspiration to Karl Marx perhaps tells us

[8] The reference is an obscure one. It is possibly a reference to Ted Sharp, ornithologist and author of *The Albino Bunting* (1991) or Eliot Sharp, fashion historian and author of *Linen Trousers* (1992). These books are now very rare. Ted Sharp vanished in Vera Cruz in 1999. Eliot Sharp is believed to have returned to Alaska in 2003.

[9] 'Another scholar who has also taken the trouble to read this obscure text': A bourgeois critic would spend many weeks tracking down this reference. For my part I simply had to reach for the third shelf down in my personal library, where the book in question, a paperback, the 1978 edition published in Melbourne, wedged between *Quelque chose noir* and *La pluralité des mondes de Lewis* and going a little yellow at the edges, contained tucked into its pages a review of its contents by George Steiner, who commented that the author 'has really written three books wrapped in one: a study of what Karl Marx read, an analysis of the ways in which his reading influenced his own written style, and a survey of Marx's theoretical and pragmatic views on literature'.

everything we need to know about this pernicious and barren trend in narrative. As the *Royal Female Magazine* noted (February 1660), Sterne's novel displays 'a contempt of all the rules observed in other writings'. That spirit of anarchy resurfaced in those governments and leaders who flouted and continue to flout the post-1945 understanding that underpins the democratic rule of law.

'The struggle between the enlightened west and its commitment to the rules-based international order and those who have launched a crusade against freedom and progress – a crusade against our way of life – exactly mirrors the struggle between the realist novel and those who seek to undermine the narrative of order and reason.

'It was that great founding father of the novel that we know today, Samuel Richardson, who perceived that *Tristram Shandy* was a gross, vulgar book full of "Uncountable wildness", provoking in any decent mind only extreme disgust. His one consolation was that its mediocrity was such that nothing could prevent it swiftly sinking into obscurity; his only anxiety was that "this ridiculous compound will be the cause of many more productions, witless and humourless, perhaps, but indecent and absurd".

'Mercifully, Richardson's prediction was partly fulfilled. *Tristram Shandy* lingers on – but few in their right minds ever read it. As for its influence, all kinds of nonsense lurks on the fringes of world literature. Whether or not Georgi Gospodinov, Yoshikichi Furui and Simon Sellars – to pluck three from a vast list of novelists unknown to readers of mature taste – ever read a word of Sterne, I have no idea. But what I do know is that the wise reader seeks a beginning, a middle, and an end, without looseness, voids, or ambiguities. Without it, darkness and anarchy beckon.'

Second standing ovation.

It takes Delphine just seven seconds to cross the conservatory. The last object she passes is a wooden cabinet containing two bottles of Armagnac from Domaine d'Espérance and some choice summer Burgundies, including a splendid Château de Meursault premier cru and a simply gorgeous Domaine de la Pousse d'Or premier cru.

Beyond this cabinet lies the ground floor lounge.

11.45am The Lounge

She pads leopard-fast across the orange rug with a pale taupe fringe upon which just a few days earlier she had called out, 'Mick! The woman from *Good Housekeeping* is here!'

That day, cloudy with a little light rain, Britain's biggest selling lifestyle magazine had sent BMW-driving Frances Doyle, twenty-seven, bubbly, attractive, highly scented, privately educated, bad at maths, an atrocious speller. Her self-confidence was diminished by her star-struck approach, which was perhaps only natural when in the presence of genius. It was assumed that not all good housekeepers would have heard of Sir Michael, and so it was necessary later, when she wrote her piece, for Ms Doyle to supply them with an introduction:

> He enters the room with quiet dignity, looking for all the world like an emeritus professor of philosophy from a top Oxford college. But this is the Barker Prize-winning novelist who has three times been the Richard and Judy Best Read of the Year and also won both the prestigious W. H. Smith Literary Award and Reader's Digest Author of the Year. In the flesh Britain's greatest living writer seems the living embodiment of his fiction – deeply thoughtful, socially aware, profoundly alert to moral issues of trust, understanding and perception.
>
> His electrifying and controversial sequence of early novels, including *Sunday Roast* – a baby, a microwave, don't ask! – created a sensation. Later he turned away from dark tales of psychological extremity to address wider questions of politics, history and society. *Restitution*, adapted as a major Hollywood film starring Carey Mulligan, won plaudits from the critics and is widely regarded as his masterpiece. His new novel *The Berlin Exit* is a moving account of a talented composer whose life crumbles when his wife becomes a leading campaigner for Brexit.
>
> Mick Owen – he waves away his title with a modest wave of his hand and a self-deprecating smile. 'I never use it,' he

confides, eyes twinkling, 'except when booking a table in a restaurant.' He laughs but then his tone suddenly becomes deadly and deeply serious. 'I accepted the knighthood not for myself but on behalf of literature. For all those who never received what was owed to them – Chaucer, Milton, Shakespeare.'

As in a scene from one of his prize-winning novels, where the choices which people make sometimes define the rest of their lives, we discuss the issue of whether to opt for tea or coffee. Mick says he is basically a tea man – Lapsang Souchong, he admits, with a wry smile – while I choose coffee.

'White or black?' he asks, with all the directness of his highly polished narratives, which have won him comparisons with literary stars like Jonathan Franzen, Jonathan Safran Foer, Jonathan Lethem, Jonathan Coe, and Jonathan Kellerman.

'White, please,' I say.

'Strong or medium?' he asks.

'Medium,' I say.

'A good centrist choice,' he quips. He names twelve varieties of coffee bean from around the world and invites me to choose. 'You understand, I am a pluralist,' he explains.

I opt for Kenyan.

'Would you like your milk cold, warmed-up in a pan, or frothy?'

I become aware of the infinite complexity of that thing we call reality.

'Cold is fine,' I say.

'Good,' he nods approvingly. 'Moderation and simplicity are the keys to a well-lived life.' Suddenly I feel that I am in the presence of a man who might have given the Buddha a tip or two. But this life-lesson in the unendingly recessive state of things is not yet over.

'Would you care for a chocolate digestive?' he suddenly asks, and I say that normally I would not but on this occasion I would like one very much. He nods at his elegant wife Delphine, who is loitering in the doorway wearing a stunning pair of Christian Louboutin suedes. Soon this most delightful and accommodating of wives can be heard in the kitchen ('It is the cook's day off,' Mick explains), expertly using a coffee grinder to transform dark gleaming beans to a rich, flavoursome chocolate-coloured dust.

As we wait for Delphine to return with a tray I glance out of the window at the garden, where over to one side of the great lawn a solar panel with the dimensions of a wing on The Angel of the North turns gently on its supporting pole.

'I have always been passionate about the environment,' Mick remarks, shrewdly noting where my gaze has fallen.

In September 2009 he signed up to the 10:10 project, which surely marked a turning point in saving the world from climate catastrophe. Mick Owen was there in person when the project's public launch was held at Tate Modern. Everyone present made a personal commitment to reduce their personal emissions. In the first three days over ten thousand celebrities, ordinary people, businesses and organisations had joined, including London Zoo and Tottenham Hotspur Football Club.

Mick has since spoken at environmental conferences around the world, flying as far afield as Tokyo, Shanghai, Sydney, Auckland, Vancouver, Toronto, Lagos, Cairo, Honolulu, Santiago, Lima, Boston, Los Angeles, Moscow and Pretoria, and to all the capital cities of the EU, to make a passionate and deeply felt appeal for everyone to take personal responsibility for reducing their carbon footprint.

The 10:10 project remains dear to his heart. He gave his enthusiastic support to the charity's Car Free Cities campaign, 'designing and delivering practical grassroots solutions', such as encouraging people to give up the car and walk and cycle. The charity makes it clear that a 'car free city' does not mean cities without cars. It is recognised that many people cannot get around without a car and sometimes there are hard choices to be made. Cycle paths cannot be accommodated where streets are used for parking, and often it is the case that owners of larger vehicles such as Range Rovers need to park across the pavement in order to let ambulances and other emergency vehicles pass. But if some drivers can be persuaded to walk or cycle then progress can be made. Mick himself drives only electric cars and has cut his personal vehicle fleet from seven to four. 'We must all make sacrifices,' he remarks. He travels with Paravel suitcases, made from recycled vegan leather, and uses private jets only when absolutely necessary.

His passion for Darwin is a perfect match for his commitment to a Greener world. He recently flew to Ecuador, then took a 500-mile flight to San Cristóbal in order to sail to the Galapagos on the Silver Origin – a vessel with a sustainable menu and energy, light and waste-management systems designed to reduce its footprint. The novelist smiles as he fondly recalls eating zero-miles ceviche as he reconnected with nature. His 'Green recharge' has so far involved trips to the Arctic, Antarctica, Sumatra and Madagascar. He is a regular both at a healing retreat near Cape Town which boasts a chakra garden and a villa on the Indonesian island of Sumba, in a complex popular with the Beckhams and Ed Sheeran. Mick winks as he assures me that the spa treatments under a thatched pagoda are 'very popular with the ladies'.

Among other successes which the 10:10 project can chalk up is Transport for London cutting the carbon emissions of ten underground stations by ten per cent by reducing escalator service at off-peak times.

Although 'on board' with the project's campaigns Mick is no longer formally associated with the charity. He cut his links after the release of the satirical short film *No Pressure*, which showed children and adults being blown up after refusing to cut their emissions. 'In very bad taste,' he says. Mick adds that he has no time for 'eco-zealots' who glue themselves to paintings or who lie down in the road and block important routes out of London. He has, he confides, been personally delayed for over two hours in the Limehouse Link because of such tactics.

It was out of this commitment and these experiences that he wrote his 'Green' novel, *Incandescent*. It is the darkly comic tale of a brilliant inventor, David Laughton, who discovers how to store solar power in highly concentrated energy packs. These packs – 'lozenges' (named after their size and shape) – offer to liberate humanity from fossil fuels. A single lozenge allows a car to be driven for ten thousand miles before requiring replacement. But before he can pass on this great gift his research laboratory is burned down by animal rights protesters, who mistake it for a factory farm chicken unit. Fleeing with his small collection of precious lozenges and his pet rabbit Hudson, Laughton finds himself pursued by Russian and Chinese secret agents, who want to steal them for their tyrannical governments to use in powering ballistic missiles. Tragically, his escape across London is delayed by eco-zealots who have blocked Westminster Bridge. This comic tale of pursuit takes place against the background of Laughton's collapsing pri-

ON MICK'S BOOKSHELF

- Celeste Ng totally blows me away. I've been immersed in her fabulous comic novel *Everything I Never Told You*. It's the compulsively readable tale of a dysfunctional mixed-race family in 1970s America. If you are ever faced by a ten-hour flight and you want an upbeat book with sharply edged characters and a plot that races along, this is the one to choose!

- Nick Cohen, *What's Left?* A devastating critique of the follies of the Left by one of the most incisive minds writing for today's liberal press. Why is Palestine a cause for so many but not North Korea? Cohen bravely asks the questions that others dare not.

- India Knight is best known as one of the finest journalists of our time. But – surprise! – she is also a remarkable novelist. *Mutton* is a profoundly wise yet sparklingly witty take on the ageing process. I devoured it in one slice! Enjoy.

vate life, as his wife leaves him for another woman, and his twin brother decides to identify as a hermaphrodite. *The Guardian* hailed *Incandescent* as 'the greatest comic writing since Kingsley Amis', while *The Washington Post* called it 'an instant classic'.

As we sip our hot drinks, Mick tells me that at one point early on in his career he suffered from a loss of confidence. 'I used to read people like Samuel Beckett and ask myself: what am I doing? I began to doubt my sentences. But then my wonderful, brilliant agent Sandra Locke – now sadly passed away – told me bluntly to forget guys like that. 'You should see Beckett's sales figures. They're crap.'

He laughs, remembering. 'And then I realised –' [cont. p. 197]

Delphine passes the stylish Svenskt Tenn lamp, the awesome indoor stone table by Axel Vervoordt and the striped pouffe made from recycled yogurt pots and plant-based Biofoam. Sunlight glints from the gilt and silver Asprey telephone which rests on the table. A mild frown ripples her brow and momentarily tugs at the corners of her mouth. When it came to décor that abominable youngster from *Good Housekeeping* had patently failed to identify high-end good taste when it stared her in the face. There had been no mention of any of these domestic embellishments in her feature – or for that matter Delphine's Bremont Lady K watch or her re-entry in black mesh Mary Janes from Jimmy Choo. Unbelievable.

As Delphine's feet depart from the Carlotta Clementine rug, the hand tufted wool briefly bears the imprint of her size three feet. When they are gone the crushed fibres rise up again, each wiry tendril like the restless, yearning penis of a lusty fourteen-year-old shortly after orgasm.

Now Delphine's bare feet can be heard beyond the doorway, skipping down the main corridor towards the central staircase.

11.46am The Corridor

This corridor connects the important ground floor rooms and is of a width seen in stately homes. It is lined with objects purchased on Mick's foreign travels, or at auctions, or found in antique shops in sleepy Cotswold villages.

Once, briefly, in his twenties, after the collapse of his first marriage, his first marriage, his first marriage...

Ah, what a tale was there!

Mick was an early riser – in every sense. As a teenager he was sexually precocious. This was unusual among the middle classes of that era, but it was his great good fortune to be in the same class as Gwynedd Hooley. She adored him, she was quietly voluptuous, her body had powerful cravings. Her breasts pressed forwards against her white regulation shirt. Buttoned, her blue blazer bulged. Her dark pleated skirt hung over her plump thighs and black stockings like a theatre curtain before the start of a performance. The play which was about to begin combined aspects of Vanbrugh, *Volpone* and Verona (The Two Gentlemen of) – with a Hampshire-angled splash of *Room at the Top*.

Mick and Gwynedd were both fifteen years old and in the same fifth form class. [10] By then he'd been a pupil at Purborough Grammar School for five years. His parents had moved from Huntingdonshire to Hampshire in 1959. His father was coming to the end of his RAF career. He had a desk job at the base on Thorney Island but his wife absolutely refused to live at the accommodation available at that desolate location. They bought a newly built bungalow on a dead-end lane in nearby Warblington, with a view of the castle tower. As a phallic symbol it was inspirational to the adolescent Mick – a spur to ambition; a colossus amid slumping barns and cattle-field torpor; a perpetual reminder of what mattered most in

[10] 'in the same fifth form class': The school records establish that this was class 5B.

life. He was thrilled years later when he saw *Tommy* and discovered that the film crew had shot some scenes in the village – including its most prominent erection.

Gwynedd Hooley lived in Havant, a town only fifteen minutes away on foot. The A27 sliced past Warblington and on in a straight line through Havant's heart, then on to Bedhampton (Keats's plaque),[11] Cosham, and the junctions for Portsmouth and Southsea. But you hardly noticed cars in those days, there were so few of them. Even the middle classes still cycled to work. There were no cheap flights abroad. Summer meant boarding a bus to Havant railway station and catching

[11] 'Keats's plaque': The plaque is attached to The Mill House, Bedhampton. On 23 January 1819 John Keats arrived at The Mill House, staying a fortnight and writing 'The Eve of St Agnes'. The following year, on 28 September 1820, a storm forced the ship that Keats was travelling on to dock at Portsmouth. He spent the night at The Mill House before returning to the vessel and proceeding to Italy, where he died five months later. His final stay at The Mill House was his last night on English soil. Once a tranquil, out-of-the-way place, The Mill House now enjoys perpetual Gothic thunder, as today it overlooks speeding motor vehicles on the multi-lane re-routed A27 main south coast highway. Questioned about this local connection to Keats, Mick Owen remarked that he had no knowledge of it at all during the years he lived with his parents at Warblington. In the 1960s his school bus followed the old A27 route, from which The Mill House was not visible. Today, visitors to Bedhampton can rest their buttocks on a special commemorative bench, the result of a collaboration between Bidbury Mead Friends and Havant Men's Shed. It bears a portrait of the poet and the words, 'Ah, silver shrine, here I will take my rest'. A member of the Bedhampton Historical Collection group said: 'John Keats was the last of the Romantic poets to be born and, sadly, the first to die.' The leader of Havant Borough Council said that it was right to recognise Keats's cultural importance to the borough and he hoped future poets would be inspired by sitting on this bench. The fact that Keats wrote his longest poem while staying in Bedhampton surely indicates the lack of anything better to do in this banal and uninteresting village which is as soporific today as it was two hundred years ago.

the Puffing Billy to Hayling Island. Back then everyone except the rich went to the seaside. Hayling beach had miles of sand, a funfair, a frontage of chalets. There were three holiday camps: Northney, Sinah Warren and Warners. Mick remembered that the entrance to one of the camps had a cream-coloured arch which seemed to be modelled on the one straddling the entrance to Universal Studios.

Havant had a grammar school but Mick's father regarded it as dangerously progressive and unsuitable for the son of an RAF employee. One wanted if at all possible to immunise one's child against the deadly infection of socialism. *The Sunday Express* cautioned against this lethal virus, which was everywhere, especially in popular music. The moral fibre of the United States of America was currently being sapped by a dangerous young woman named Joan Baez, whose musical recordings were available in the United Kingdom. Therefore Owen senior selected Purborough Grammar School as a superior choice for the education of his only child. Purborough lay beyond Portsmouth, out of sight behind the South Downs, in a fold of woodland and meadows. Purborough's headmaster, Charles Edward Lemon, believed in order and discipline. Corporal punishment was a regular feature of school life. Charles Edward Lemon liked nothing better than to see a male child bending over a chair in his office. Grey fabric stretched over immaculate young buttocks caused powerful feelings to churn at his body's fork. *Crack!* went his cane. Again. Again. Again. Again. Again. Sex – six, rather – of the best. Whipping a miscreant always left him flushed and requiring a change of underwear.

A double-decker school bus lumbered westward every morning from the West Sussex border, collecting the children whose parents felt that Havant Grammar was inferior to Purborough Grammar. It was on this bus that Mick met Richard Kane of Emsworth, who became his friend between the ages of eleven and eighteen. Gwynedd Hooley also rode this bus, although they never sat next to each other because boys rode the upper deck and girls stayed below.

Each Saturday afternoon, just after lunch, Richard Kane cycled to Warblington and then he and Mick went on to the public library in Havant. Its non-fiction shelves implicitly challenged the category, featuring books about flying saucers, haunted rectories and the Loch Ness Monster. The most enticing title in fiction was *The Naked and the Dead* – a title to titillate, a title to make you tingle – but Mick knew he would never have the courage to take it up to the counter and get it stamped by Miss Hawk.

Commandant of the library, Miss Hawk was white-haired and ancient. Her mouth was a fixed scowl, her nose beak-shaped. She shushed and hissed and was always calling for silence. The library was as cold and quiet as a marble mausoleum. Miss Hawk, like other librarians, possessed far more photoreceptors than ordinary humans. She had an indented fovea and extraordinarily acute hearing.

Mick settled for *Mariners of Space*, a ripping yarn about Colin Devenish, a Space-Ranger of the Interplanetary Force. Colin sets off from 'the vast Space Fort of Croydon' to do battle with the evil Karl Vaanus, who threatens to plunge the solar system into war. *Croydon*. Wasn't that where Dirk Bogarde once shot a film? Autumn leaves, wide empty streets, a gloomy old house with a large garden...

In those golden days dustjackets helpfully supplied the plot and the ending: 'They play hide-and-seek in the firmament until the better man wins. The threat of war is averted, and Space-Captain Devenish settles down to enjoy the amenities of twenty-first-century England.'

After choosing their books Mick and Richard pedalled back to Kane's house, where they watched the Saturday afternoon wrestling show. Big beefy men in leotards. They had names like Bruiser Bill and Slammer Sid. They snarled at each other before the match began. On cue, the audience roared; booed; applauded. As they clashed Bruiser and Slammer grunted and groaned like lovers ripped by orgasm. Eventually (as in any romance) one of the men soared over the other and landed with a crash. The audience went wild. It was several years before Mick's consciousness had developed to that advanced state where he finally realised these shows were a fraud. It had been decided beforehand who was The Bad Man and who The Good Wrestler. The snarling was the performance of amateur actors. The fights were choreographed. It was basically *Hamlet* without the speeches and the supporting cast.

One day Richard was ill and so Mick cycled to the library alone. As he approached, who should be walking past but Gwynedd Hooley! Her coat was as scarlet as his headgear, and both were woollen. She greeted him warmly and made no comment on his Tam o' Shanter, which rested at a rakish angle on his head. It had been a gift from his Uncle Harry, who had recently returned from a faraway exotic city called Edinburgh.

Gwynedd explained that she lived nearby. Her parents were out but he was welcome to come round for a biscuit. Mick accepted the invitation. The sequence of events which led from a chocolate finger to tender nervous fingering to boldly exposed genitals can be safely left to the lusty reader to visualise. The only third-party witness was Amelia, the Hooley family's labrador. At one point she licked Mick's bottom, which he found strangely exciting. But he pushed the lascivious bitch away when Amelia pressed her wet nose against his anus and then enthusiastically began to sniff his testicles. The dog might almost have been the reincarnation of Philip Roth, were it not for the fact that he'd published only two novels by this date and would live for another fifty-five years.

In short, Mick mounted Gwynedd and afterwards his bicycle. He returned to Warblington without a library book, sweating. He explained that this week there was nothing that appealed to him. He was done with George Adamski's adventures, poltergeist activity in Essex and shy amphibious dinosaurs which led a quiet existence down the road from Inverness. And Norman Mailer's *The Deer Park* had been a great disappointment. He had hoped it might be about Petworth.

After that memorable occasion Saturday was his busiest day of the week. Every morning Gwynedd's parents went shopping and Mick pedalled over to her house. They fucked twice, then he went home for lunch. In the afternoon he went to the library with Richard Kane and then watched the wrestling.

It was a mystery why Gwynedd didn't get pregnant earlier than she did. It was a week before his seventeenth birthday that the inevitable occurred. Gwynedd's parents unexpectedly arrived at Mick's home on Sunday afternoon. Her father was trembling with anger, her mother was red-eyed, with tear-streaked cheeks. They broke the news of their daughter's impending motherhood.

Mick's father dragged him from his bedroom and forced out a public confession. In sisterhood, Mick's mother also began weeping. The two fathers glared at Mick as if he were an insolent native in a colony or a Balmoral butler who had just powerfully farted in close proximity to the sovereign's nostrils.

'Since they were both fifteen years old!' sobbed Mrs Hooley, scarcely believing it to be possible.

'Filthy little swine,' snarled Mr Hooley. His sound and fury greatly resembled Bruiser Bill's before Round One.

'How could you, Michael?' his mother whimpered. (Quite easily, mother. Gwynedd took the matter in hand and guided me in until I got the hang of it.)

The Montagues and the Capulets it wasn't. Peace was quickly and smoothly established with a shotgun marriage. Mick and Gwynedd would forgo a church wedding and a white dress. Havant registry office would suffice. The main thing was the child wouldn't be a bastard. That would have been the final shame.

Gwynedd gave up school and stayed at home to swell. Her new husband would continue his education but would henceforth live with his new in-laws. There, the atmosphere was even more glacial than at the library. Mick Owen was a major disappointment. He had not been the kind of husband they had planned for Gwynedd. They had anticipated a man some ten years older, with a solid job. A bank manager, say.

And then Gwynedd miscarried. The marriage had been for nothing. And now everyone was stuck with it. The only consolation was that Gwynedd and Mick could have licenced sex every day of the week. But from this copious transfer of semen came no further fertilisation.

Mick did his 'A' levels, obtaining a B in Geography, an E in History and a D in English Literature. You couldn't hope to get into university with grades like those. He became a clerical officer for the Civil Service, working at the Havant Labour Exchange. This operated out of a new office block, two storeys high, on the other side of the tracks to Havant station. The staff went in at one end, the clients at the other. It was the golden age of filing cabinets, and much of Mick's day was spent removing brown folders from a filing drawer, passing them to much older colleagues at their desks, and taking other files back to their metallic nests.

Once a week he dealt directly with the unemployed. One by one their names were called. They approached the counter and Mick asked each person – usually male, but there was a scattering of women – if they were still unemployed. If they said Yes – they always said Yes – he took his rubber stamp, pressed it into an ink pad, and stamped UNEMPLOYED against each of the seven days of the week. The client then signed the slip, which was placed in his brown folder. Mick then gave another slip to the client to take to another clerical officer further along the counter. A few years later, when he went for the first time into Foyles bookshop on Charing Cross Road, Mick experienced a strong sense of déjà vu. In Foyles in those days the purchase of a book involved a complicated bureaucratic procedure which seemed to indicate that the business did not trust its staff with cash and that customers required punishment for their neediness.

Mick's most embarrassing moment was when he had to call out the name of an unfortunate whose surname was Bastard. He did his best, avoiding bars and tarred roads and instead matching sea bass with Tadcaster.

It was during this barren phase of his life – richly sensual between the sheets yet domestically cramped and oppressive – that Mick began to write his first novel. At the parental home in Warblington the only books on the shelves were his mother's crime novels and his father's titles about bombers, fighter planes, and RAF history. Mick quite liked crime, coasting through the works of Ngaio Marsh, Agatha Christie and Josephine Tey. But they opened no windows into his own imagination. In the Hooley household it was different. Gwynedd's parents were Havant intellectuals. They adored the novels of Nevil Shute and Daphne du Maurier. Gwynedd progressed to the works of Edna O'Brien and Françoise Sagan. In his earliest interviews as a young and successful writer Mick paid tribute to his much loved in-laws and his adorable wife. Without their fine taste in literature he would never have grasped the central importance of plot and characterisation to any narrative worth reading.

Scribble, scribble, scribble. Tap, tap, tappety-tap. In the evenings he retreated to the bedroom, while his wife sat downstairs with her parents watching 'This Is Your Life'. Scribble, scribble, scribble. Tap, tap, tappety-tap.

'Where do your ideas come from?' That was what fans at book signings frequently enquired. It was a good question. At first he was flummoxed. He supposed it was a mixture of personal experience, the books he'd read, the films he'd seen. Imaginary narratives framed the shape and content of his life so far. The example of existing narratives suffused his own.

Later, annoyed to be asked yet again, he'd retort, 'A storage depot on an industrial estate in Leyton.'

His first novel poured out of him – raw, urgent, unpolished, passionate, intense. Only three people knew he was writing it. His in-laws regarded the idea as inherently preposterous and a patently false reason for spending so much time alone in the bedroom. They suspected unnatural practices. Gwynedd was simply uninterested. Why read an unpublished story in an ungainly format when you can read a paperback? Besides, she knew Mick would never write anything that moved her the way *Bonjour Tristesse* did.

Once his tale was complete he bought *The Writers' and Artists' Yearbook* and posted the top copy, saving the precious carbon. In those days you could submit direct to a publisher.

After fifteen rejections he became depressed.

Next he tried a literary agent. 'Dear Curtis,' he began.

But Curtis Brown did not reply in person. Instead it was a woman called Jemima who signed the letter saying that his manuscript was not really for them. She added a tip. They were looking for the new Jean Plaidy. She recommended that Mick read some of her novels.

The next name he plucked from the list was Sandra Locke's. He didn't know it but Sandra Locke had left Curtis Brown, acrimoniously, and was just starting out as an independent. By now Mick was nineteen. He was into his second year as a civil servant. Gwynedd, still not pregnant, had started working behind the bar at The Bear on East Street.

Sandra Locke asked to see the manuscript – by now dog-eared, crumpled, coffee-stained and faintly scented with nicotine. Mick went to the Post Office and sent it off.

Three days later her reply dropped through the letterbox. Sandra Locke thought his novel was terrific. She would very much like to meet him with a view to representation. Could he telephone in order to arrange a visit to her London office?

Her disembodied voice was husky and rough as sandpaper. She sounded like Simone Signoret in *Room at the Top*. Mick applied for a day off work and took a fast train to Waterloo. He negotiated the mysteries of the London Underground and managed to arrive on time at the address in pre-fashionable Spitalfields. Like all literary agencies the office was on the second floor of an unimpressive and anonymous building on a busy road. He toiled up a cold stairwell on steps which creaked, carefully avoiding tongues of curling linoleum.

Her office door was frosted glass, like a private detective's in a Chandler story. Mick pressed a button, a bell shrilled, beyond the glass a dark shape flickered forward. A tall thin girl dressed in black; her secretary, Jane.

Sandra Locke sat swathed in smoke behind a desk piled with manuscripts. The room was lined with bookshelves, where the books were stacked vertically, twelve titles high.

She had cleared a space on her desk. Mick recognised his battered manuscript, which sat at the centre, like a rectangular spacecraft just descended into a lunar crater.

'Cigarette?'

Mick declined.

'Whisky?'

He glanced at his wristwatch. It was not yet noon. He was rather shocked that anyone should be drinking whisky in the morning. But he knew he had to please this woman, who was interested in his writing. 'Please,' he said.

She poured him a generous amount.

'Dettol,' she said.

He was too inexperienced to get the joke. It was only when he sampled the Laphroaig that he half-understood. It had a peculiar and distinctive taste.

In later years he never was much of a spirits man. In tribute to George Orwell he occasionally bought Jura, but that was for guests. The only whisky he had much time for was Aberlour. But just occasionally, on very special occasions, he'd reach for his green bottle of forty-year-old Laphroaig.

Sandra pointed at his manuscript. 'This is bloody good.' She sucked on her foul-smelling French cigarette. 'You have the gift.'

Mick grunted. It was a trick he'd learned while on holiday with his parents in Dorset. Their bed and breakfast had been adjacent to a pig farm.

'Tell me something about yourself.'

He gave her the basics.

After that they moved on to his manuscript. He told her what Jemima had said about Jean Plaidy.

'Fuck Jean Plaidy. You're no Jean Plaidy and you never will be. You're *you*. You're the voice of change. Youth. A new perspective on life. Dark, ironic. Bleak. There's a market for this. The business just doesn't know it yet. You know who runs publishing houses? I'll tell you. Old men who went to Wellington College and then Oxford. Their dream authors are Evelyn fucking Waugh and Anthony fucking Powell.'

She said: 'I want to sign you. I'm going to make you *huge*.'

Sandra was a disappointment, physically. He had dreamed of a sexy siren, experienced and hungry for new experience. Alas, Sandra Locke was unattractive – a squashed-up woman with a large waist, rather saggy breasts, bags under her eyes, thick features. Before working for CB she'd been at Faber. She'd known T. S. Eliot. 'I'll tell you the secret of success,' she said gruffly. 'Networking.' She grinned, which made her face crack open with creases and their tributaries. 'Plus talent.'

She indicated his manuscript. 'Of course it will need some work. It needs editing. Leave that to me.'

She liked the title. *In Bed with Emily*. It teased and titillated. 'Sex sells,' she confided, tapping ash. 'Sexual knowledge – that's something everyone is interested in. Nobody wants to feel they're missing out. It's important to find out what other people are up to.'

She laughed. 'As for the twist... That's bloody brilliant. A knock-out.'

Everyone knows about it now. But back then first-time readers naturally assumed that Emily was a girl. The hero – a lusty youth of nineteen – falls madly in love with Emily. Her big brown eyes bewitch him. Her desire to please him is boundless. Her tongue drips with affection. It is only after the relationship becomes sexual that the reader discovers that Emily is a black Labrador.

The plot was perfect, the characters needed a bit more colour. Sandra taught Mick the virtue of short sentences. Chop up the rhythm. Don't bore the reader. No digressions. Give them suspense and withhold knowledge, then, a little later, dole out the information.

He was nineteen when Sandra signed him up. Her basic cut was fifteen per cent. It was worth it. She spent six months polishing the text, then sold it for a handsome advance to Genevieve Carp. It was a two-book deal. He had to deliver the next novel by the end of 1971. Carp embarked on a major marketing campaign. Mick Owen – Britain's finest young writer.

With the advance they were able to move out of the Hooley house and into a one-bedroom flat over the betting shop on North Street, Mick and Gwynedd's first real home. But the advance didn't cover the cost of living – rent, a new TV, a washing machine, bills, food and drink. Mick continued to work at the Labour Exchange and Gwynedd stayed on at The Bear.

In Bed with Emily was published on his twenty-first birthday. It was a sensation. 'It does for bestiality what *Lolita* did for paedophilia,' said the *Guardian*, admiringly. George Millar in the *Daily Express* saw it as a mockery of the standard romantic novel. He called the book 'astonishingly risqué, brilliantly satirical, oddly moving'. 'Tender, daring, humane, simply amazing,' chimed the *New York Times*. Translation rights were sold across Europe.

When Gwynedd finally read the book in proof she was horrified. 'But Emily is Amelia! Oh Mick, how could you! You haven't – you didn't – tell me it isn't true.'

'Of course it isn't true. It's a work of fiction. It's all made up.'

'Daddy will never believe you.'

Moments like these give birth to shrugs – tiny but very strong creatures much resembling lice but wholly transparent. They exist as twins, one in each human shoulder. The exact mechanism remains a mystery but it is the case that a certain sequence of words, usually but not always dialogue, causes them to nip certain muscles, causing both shoulders to rise up at the same time.

Gwynedd's prediction was correct. Her father told Mick *In Bed with Emily* was disgusting filth and he never wanted him in their house again. Leaving aside the bestiality and nightmare visions of those occasions when Mick had been alone in the house with Amelia, *In Bed with Emily* was plainly set in a thinly disguised Havant ('a town devoid of character, with a population to match, straddling the main Portsmouth-London railway line'). The subplot involved a depraved librarian, a drug-taking bank manager, and a promiscuous headmaster, set against a background of witchcraft and animal sacrifice. Mr Hooley rather felt that the drug-taking bank manager was based upon himself.

The film rights to *In Bed with Emily* were sold for a sum far exceeding Mick's advance from Genevieve Carp. It meant that he was finally able to give up working at the Labour Exchange and dedicate himself to writing full-time. He encouraged Gwynedd to continue at The Bear, not because they needed the money but because it kept her out of the house. To write, he required solitude and silence. He did not want regular enquiries about any need he might have for a digestive biscuit and a nice cup of tea. He did not wish to hear the wild rumble of a foam-filled drum swirling his smalls. If he needed background noise then a Bach or Mozart LP would do nicely.

He raced through a first draft of *Loving Lulu* and despatched it to Spitalfields. Sandra looked at his next manuscript and communicated the depressing news that she thought it was awful. She said he needed mentoring. She negotiated an extra year with Genevieve Carp and through her connections got Mick a place at the University of East Anglia. He would study for a degree in Creative Writing under the tutelage of Angus Wilson and Alan Burns. 'Wilson will help with style and with humour. Burns doesn't sell but he'll open your mind to experiment. Of the two, Wilson is the one to take notice of. Be careful with Burns. If you want to sell, watch your accessibility. Readers don't like to have to work. They want to relax.'

'What about Malcolm Bradbury?'

Sandra snorted. 'My dear boy, the campus novel is a genre in which university professors look at themselves in mirrors. It's a dead end. More to the point, it's a niche market. Niche markets are for losers. If you want to succeed you need to appeal to people who read the *Mail*. Think big.'

In September of that year, 1971, he moved with his wife to Norwich, taking an upstairs flat on the Unthank Road. It was almost opposite a bakery, where Gwynedd swiftly obtained work. Each morning he set off to walk to the University, along quiet leaf-strewn residential streets.

He didn't know it at the time but it marked the end of his first marriage.

*

Once, briefly, in his twenties, after the collapse of his relationship with Gwynedd, Mick lived alone in a rented room. Though small it was large enough to contain his most important possessions: an Olympia Portable de Luxe typewriter, a dozen long playing records (Dylan, The Incredible String Band, Fairport Convention during Sandy Denny's residency), around thirty paperbacks, mainly Penguins. But that was then and then came later. Later, after the collapse of his second marriage, he became seriously wealthy. Rich, he became a collector. Once, in the earliest days of his career, he had extravagantly praised John Fowles's first novel *The Collector*, identifying it as by far the novelist's finest work.[12] In a flash of radicalism Mick asserted that property was theft and collecting was an addiction indulged in by the morally blank bourgeoisie.

Decades later he had no memory of ever expressing such sentiments.

Delphine sprints along a corridor lined with Victorian busts of Plato, Aristotle, Socrates and other Greek celebs. There are huge striped vases the size of Ali Baba oil jars. There are large framed photographs of moments from Mick's epic career. One rainy day image shows him hooded, in a duffel coat, at the entrance to the old Bloomsbury offices of Genevieve Carp. In another, much older now, he is on a stage, accepting a medal from an old bald man wearing a Chamberlain collar and a bow tie.

Nearby there is a barely noticeable rectangle of discolouration where a frame has been removed. Once it showed Mick in a cluttered book-lined office, deep in conversation with his editor, Tim Fischer. But Fischer, once a valued associate, has fallen into disfavour. In 2004 Tim Fischer published *Top Dog: My*

[12] 'by far the novelist's finest work': An obviously absurd judgement. Fowles, however, noted the compliment and duly returned it, hailing *Loving Lulu* as 'astonishing and impressive'.

Life in Publishing. It was a long essay in self-congratulation, peppered with bitchy anecdotes about famous authors and their multiple inadequacies.

When Sam Quiggly read *Top Dog* he laughed hollowly. The author had attempted to position himself as the detached and sophisticated observer of the follies of the famous. He claimed affectionate amusement at the innumerable failings he had witnessed. Yet beneath the purported bonhomie bubbled a seething sewer of malice.

It was evident that Tim Fischer was consumed by ancient slights and grudges. These repeatedly included occasions from decades earlier when, after a meal, individuals whom Fischer strongly felt should have picked up the bill chose to ignore it until Fischer himself felt sullenly obliged to pay. The anger still burned brightly after all this time. Those particular anecdotes made Sam's face twist into what a literary bestseller would call *a savage sneer*. Years earlier, in his role as Mick Owen's newly appointed official biographer, he distinctly remembered twice meeting Fischer for lunch at upmarket restaurants chosen by the great editor. Genevieve Carp were going to publish the British edition of the book. On each occasion, when the bill was laid on the table on a silver tray with two peppermints, the famous editor had snatched up the candy then excused himself, saying he had an urgent meeting to attend in Chelsea (the first time) and Mayfair (the second time). The size of the bill – Tim Fischer had very expensive tastes where wine was concerned – left Sam ashen-faced and embittered.

But the intensity of Sam's scorn and anger was only seven per cent of Mick's. In his pages Tim Fischer made no mention of a miserable nonentity like Sam Quiggly, whose name rang no bells for British readers, and produced only the tiniest of tinkles among highly educated literary-magazine-subscribing American ones. The same could not be said of the subject of Sam's projected *magnum opus*.

Top Dog contained three indiscreet pages simply entitled 'Mick Owen'. Fischer boasted how he alone had first discovered *In Bed with Emily* (not mentioning Sandra Locke or her work on the manuscript). He intimated that Owen, though possessed of talent, had required the services of an editor. He hinted that he, Tim Fischer, was first responsible for polishing the novelist's often ragged and coarse paragraphs into the glittering prize-winning prose for which he was now famous.

He described encounters with Mick's first two wives. Gwynedd was 'chubby' and 'perhaps not the brightest of women'. During dinner at Fischer's home in Powys Square he reported that she had spent much of the evening quietly weeping. She and Mick had had a row. As for 'Dippy' Scott... She was 'tall, beautiful and unquestionably a fully enfranchised citizen of La La Land'. Dippy believed that the pyramids of Egypt secretly transmitted cosmic energy to visiting spacecraft from other planets. Fischer confided that he found himself baffled as to her hold over Mick. 'One could almost believe that witches still existed, with charms to overwhelm the most rational of men.'

But that marriage, very sadly, had also soured. 'Today he is very happily married to his third wife, Delphine Diderot, a former television journalist. Everyone in publishing fervently hopes that Mick has at last found a wife who can bear to live with him!'

Fischer concluded his affectionate memoir with the story of how after Mick had won the Barker Prize the two men had dined together at The Ivy (the original celebrity-stuffed one, near Charing Cross Road). Tim Fischer wrote that he naturally expected Mick, who had just pocketed a £100,000 prize, a success which owed everything to Tim's enduring guidance and editorial finesse, would pay. But when the bill arrived at the table Mick had casually glanced at his watch, exclaimed in synthetic, carefully planned dismay, and rushed out of the restaurant, brusquely explaining over his retreating shoulder that there was a cab waiting outside to take him to Broadcasting House.

*

As she hurries along this familiar corridor Delphine pays no attention to its contents or its remarkable absences.

There are, for example, no framed photographs of Mick in conversation with his future biographer.

Nor are there any of his father-in-law, even though Ferdinand Diderot is a French intellectual of some considerable distinction.

Obviously there are no pictures of his two earlier wives.

Books are there, though, lined up neatly along frequently dusted shelves.

Mick Owen, born 1948. But not everyone born in 1948 has made it through to this particular year in the twenty-first century (which precise year will not be divulged until later, at a moment calculated to make the most impact on the enthralled reader). Some did not even make it to the end of 1969. No. The bookshelves which line this corridor hold none of the books found in Fred Hampton's apartment, after his assassination. Has Mick even *heard* of Fred Hampton? Possibly not. When he and his cronies – Marty, Jools, Tim, Tom, Craig – talk at the dinner table of 'The Hamptons' they are obviously not alluding to an obscure black family in Chicago. Nor – it goes without saying – and what's unsaid lies like a rotting corpse below the shaped marble solidity of the said. Begin again. Nor, on these shelves, it goes without saying, is there a copy of Richard Stern's book *The Books in Fred Hampton's Apartment* (Hamish Hamilton, 1974).

Harold Bloom called John Updike 'a minor novelist with a major style' – Mick winced at that – and David Foster Wallace famously described him as 'a penis with a thesaurus'. Richard Stern was sterner – or at any rate, equally scathing. Reviewing *Couples* (1968) he observed that 'The whole strikes one as a distended, strophulous version of *Appointment in Samarra*, whose prolific, self-indulgent and abusing author Updike resembles more and more.' He concluded: 'The rot of this fancy, sweating, deformed, profoundly trivial book is a public lesson for a number of us.' In *The New York Times* he returned to the attack, calling Updike's novel 'poetic slime'.

No surprise to discover that Stern adored Sterne. 'What about *Tristram Shandy*?' he asked readers of this latter newspaper. 'Isn't it an open invitation to say anything? Yes, but its energy and pathos constantly retrieve its "waste matter". And, furthermore, it doesn't keep making concessions to the standard novels of its day.' But who is this guy Stern? Some sort of academic. The unusual sort, who tracks down writers for conversation, casually remarking: 'I myself used to see Pound about once a week from November to March in 1962-1963. It was a cold winter in Venice; Pound was in bad shape, recovering from surgery, teeth not fixed, feeling the cold. He talked little, but now and then opened up and made jokes.' Upon meeting the great poet, Stern asked: 'How are you, Mr Pound?' 'Senile,' replied Pound.

Also a novelist, Richard Stern. The enduring text, *Other Men's Daughters*. Married academic with children falls deeply in love with young student. Sounds autobiographical. But no one will ever write a biography of Richard Stern, will they? No market for that, not even a niche one.

On the lowest shelf of all – Delphine had instructed their marvellous cleaning lady, Gladys (a person of colour, incidentally) never to dust these books – Mick's Roths. Signed. Delphine, usually a genial and accommodating woman, would not permit them to be shelved any higher. Gladys's brisk brushing was banned, not, as you might expect, for fear of damage – far from it – but the reverse. Delphine would have liked to witness the author's *oeuvre* gently vanish and rot under a crust of dust and the sprinkled shells of dead woodlice. Nor would the wife permit the husband to display his seven photographs of the two authors together. Phil and Mick on a bench in St James's Park. Phil and Mick, deep in conversation, holding champagne flutes at a publisher's party. Phil and Mick wearing winter coats, on the shore of a lake; in the distance someone paddling a canoe. Phil and Mick walking towards the photographer on a street in New York. Phil and Mick in an American diner; on the table, squat thick-rimmed white china coffee cups on matching saucers. Phil and Mick in close-up, wearing shirts and ties, both smiling broadly. Phil and Mick standing outside the headquarters of Aimless House in Manhattan. These treasures were kept in a folder in Mick's filing cabinet.

Delphine's animus had an origin.

That evening at their mews house in Knightsbridge.

The evening that Philip Roth and Claire Bloom came for supper.

Roth was a swaying, fully uncurled penis perpetually in search of openings. At first he was all charm. But when he followed Delphine into the kitchen – *Here, let me help you with those* – he propositioned her. 'We should get together when our spouses are out of town,' he leered, with a lecherous wink.

Spouse rhymes with house but also with louse.

Back at the table, Claire seemed edgy.

There was an explosion of temper on Roth's part when she spilled her wine. 'For Christ's sake, you stupid bitch!'

The quartet fell silent, three of them shocked and embarrassed by Roth's ugly explosion of anger. They watched the wine as it slowly crept across the cloth. Mick was reminded of his supper with the Prince of Wales.

Delphine said, 'I'll get a cloth.' She added brightly for Claire's sake, 'It's not a problem.' She forced out more consolation. 'I've always hated this tablecloth!'

A moment later she was back, dabbing at the sodden fabric.

Claire looked about to cry but succeeded in regaining her composure. She said in a low whispery voice: 'Sorry. Butterfingers.'

Roth continued to glare. He drummed on a dry section of tablecloth with his right hand. The knuckles were thick with black simian hair. A gorilla's hand. This was the hand which had written *Portnoy's Complaint*. You could not help but wonder about the slippery adventurous past of those big stubby fingers.

Mick, a diplomat to his toenails, quickly diverted them. 'Butterfingers. The etymology of that term is fascinating,' he said. 'It originally meant a clumsy archer – one who misses the target entirely. Derived from "butt" or "target", which was an abbreviation of "embankment" – the place for holding targets.'

Having enlightened them he smiled his grand smile, the one which shone with quiet intelligence and superior knowledge. Mick was pleasantly aware of Delphine gazing at him adoringly. She had always been astonished at the extraordinary breadth of his knowledge of language, literature, history, biology, zoology, astronomy, geography, psychology, cinema, popular music, classical music, painting and politics. Like Wikipedia there was nothing he did not seem to know and understand, in real depth. It was no wonder the Germans had recently given him The European Man of the Year Award. *Mick Owen's novels elegantly express the dilemmas of modern man in an age of intolerance and unreason, addressing with acute psychological profundity the difficulties of relationships in contemporary society, framed as they are by an enduring struggle between progressive and democratic liberal values and the hostile forces of irrationality, ignorance and narrow nationalism. His fiction has brought a masterly* Weltanschauung *to such topics as robots, cannibalism, incest, global warming, impossible wives and extremists of both the Left and the Right. He is without question the living incarnation of European liberalism.*

In the silence that followed Mick realised he had more to say. He continued. 'Butterfingers has nothing at all to do with a yellow substance used in the lubrication of toast or to add a dash to boiled potatoes. Etymologically it is remote from buttercups, butterflies, butterscotch or the word originally used as a store-room for liquor.'

'You'd need a big one of those when Claire is around,' Roth muttered. His eyes shone dangerously.

Then, suddenly, it was over. His bad mood evaporated, like a silver raindrop on the bonnet of a Mercedes E-Class 300CE Coupe as the sun rises over Cannes.

They all laughed and their laughter was as fragile as a house of cards, as delicate as sleigh bells in snowbound Moscow, 1916.

There followed dessert, conversation, the cheeseboard, conversation, liqueurs, conversation, coffee, some last acidic reflections on other writers and their sundry inadequacies and the poor sales and reviews suffered by those wretches. Finally, as the bawdy hand of the clock stretched towards midnight, it was time for the celebs to depart.

Claire hugged Mick and planted a full-bodied kiss on his right cheek. He felt a quick sharp tingle of pleasure. It was surely time to watch *The Spy Who Came In From The Cold* again – by far the best of the le Carré adaptations.

Next Claire hugged Delphine. Her kiss was a brisker affair, with forty-two per cent less saliva.

While this was going on Philip was pumping Mick's hand, telling him what a marvellous evening it had been. Mick at first flinched, for Roth was squeezing him just a little too hard, as Delphine sometimes did when she gave him a hand job. But as the pain receded he beamed. He knew it was true. Everything was perfect – the food, the wine, the conversation. Two giants of world literature and their attendant goddesses. This thought led on to a memory of the statue of Shakespeare in the still existing garden of that long demolished house in Stratford. Shakespeare looking deep in thought, while bare-breasted women clustered around him like celestial groupies. Sadly, his mulberry tree was gone, wilfully cut down, just like the trees George Orwell planted in his garden at Wallington.

Philip meanwhile was hugging Delphine. Mick turned to reach for the visitors' coats. Philip wore a trench coat from Gieves & Hawkes – he was very English in his tailoring choices. In its understated raspberry shade Claire's stylish Burberry coat elegantly matched her semi-quilted Saint Laurent bag.

While Mick's back was turned Philip embraced Delphine. He placed both hands lightly against her spine while meeting her lips full on. She gasped in surprise, supplying a small oval aperture leading into the cavern of her mouth. He was expecting it. His tongue slid inside her and began playfully to consort with hers. Its motions were amorous and urgent. She started to choke and reached to push him away. But his left arm had tightened, clamping her firm breasts to the unyielding Berlin wall of his chest, flattening them slightly. Roth's right hand meanwhile had set off on an excursion of its own. It slid under Delphine's belt and wormed its way down to her panties. At first there were five organs of attack but now his hand had clenched itself into a half fist, leaving his forefinger thrust out like a small, fully erect penis. It found its way into the crack between her buttocks, burrowing deeper. A moment later and his fingertip had reached her anus. She felt the pressure of his hot driven bud of flesh. Her tightening sphincter was no match for the savage power of its thrust. It dipped deep into her rectum. (What was it Suleika Dawson had said about lusty John le Carré? *He drove into me like a ploughshare.*) Delphine gasped in shock and pain.

Then, suddenly, it was over. Roth's forefinger withdrew at speed, mission accomplished, like an American special forces unit operating deep behind enemy territory. His hand was out of her underwear, back over the border marked by her leather belt, and he was disengaging his chest. His tongue, too, had returned to its homeland.

Delphine became aware that Claire had seen everything and Mick nothing. Claire looked desperately miserable. Her eyes brimmed. But she managed to croak a wretched whispery goodbye. Roth, for his part, was ebullient, larger than life. He seemed to have swelled in size (and one part of him unquestionably had). Delphine felt his eyes bore into her.

'Hoping to see *much more of you* soon!' he shouted. He directed the central portion of that aspiration towards Delphine. She flushed.

Roth raised his hand, as if in farewell. But his forefinger lingered a moment below his left nostril while he inhaled the earthy fragrance which clung to the skin. He knew he would not wash this hand for at least a week. It would be a busy and energetic week for his old five-limbed friend.

When the door closed behind them Delphine hissed, 'That man is never coming here again! *Never!* He's a monster! A perve! A filthy old lech!'

She told Mick what had occurred and his narrow eyes grew narrower. He swivelled, appalled. A shudder ran through him, then returned, limping, by a slightly different route.

'Good Lord.' He thought about it. 'Well, he does have a reputation.'

He thought some more and grinned. 'I suppose you should be flattered.'

Strangely, Delphine seemed upset by his response. She ran off to take a shower. Later, when he suggested sex, she retorted that she was not in the mood, and turned her back on him.

Moments like those were rare. Next day he flew her to Paris. They stayed at the Hotel Ritz. She visited her troubled, difficult father. Later, they dined at Le Meurice Alain Ducasse. Mick took her to the opera, to Versailles, to Père Lachaise to see the graves of Frédéric Chopin, Honoré de Balzac, Alphonse Daudet, Georges-Eugène Haussmann, Georges Moustaki, Victor Noir, Georges Perec, Camille Pissarro, Eugène Pottier, Marcel Proust, Raymond Roussel, Georges-Pierre Seurat, Simone Signoret, Joseph Spiess, Maurice Thorez, Claude-Alexandre Ysabeau, and Achille Zavatta.

She forgave him. As a mark of her favour she slipped on a pair of fishnet stockings and thigh-length leather boots and was waiting for him on the bed, rump upward, as he emerged pink and naked from the shower.

Through the window the distant Eiffel Tower winked its approval.

Later Claire wrote *A Doll's House* and her ex wrote *I Married a Communist*.

Nothing is more fun than seeing a celebrity couple transmute the gold of their ancient passion into dust and acid! Alchemy in reverse! And that is the wonderful thing about literature nowadays. Gossip has displaced critical analysis. Gossip is compelling, satisfying, extremely pleasurable. Much more interesting than what a writer writes. Who cares about invented people? Real ones are so much more interesting. Not even the finest page of prose has the interest of John le Carré's sex life – *phwooaaar!*

*

Delphine reaches the foot of the grand staircase.

The screams are funnelled down it, step by carpeted step.

11.46am The Grand Staircase

It's an original feature, this massive staircase. Broad marble steps leading upward to the first-floor landing, then curling round to meet the second floor and then the third, the grey-black dappled marble exposed at each step end.

Mick Owen. Not yet quite dead, by the sound of it. There is still vital oxygen in his lungs and he is emitting sounds of quite considerable volume.

But inside this house it is as if he were a long dead classic author. The more you see of it, the more you recognise a shrine to a lifetime of success.

Delphine sees none of this. Her mind is elsewhere. Even her nudity is forgotten. The space above her is a blur. She doesn't take in that impressive pair of framed matching photographs, massively enlarged, which hang on the walls, flanking this luxurious staircase. On the left, the actress Carey Mulligan, on the right the actor Rory Kinnear, instantly recognisable from key scenes in the 2006 smash-hit adaptation of what is widely acknowledged as Mick's masterpiece, *Restitution*. As everyone knows, the book, set just after the outbreak of war in 1914, takes place in a country house and involves twin sisters, Juliet and Jemima, and a gardener named Lawrence. During a country house party at the sisters' family home in Kent many items are stolen, including a valuable diamond necklace. When the police are called they search the house and estate and discover the stolen items in Lawrence's cottage. Apart from the stolen items there are also maps of the Kent coast and scribbled notes about local troop encampments. Lawrence is given the option of a trial for espionage or service in a front line regiment. He chooses the latter and is awarded the Military Cross for bravery at Passchendaele. Juliet, who volunteers as a nurse, runs into him in France, and they hastily marry. But Lawrence is later killed on the Somme and Juliet dies giving birth to their son, who is named Maurice. He later becomes a major poet, forever haunted by thoughts of the parents he never knew.

But in a brilliant final twist (borrowed from the end of John Updike's *Marry Me*) it emerges that these destinies are fantasy, invented by Jemima. In reality Lawrence was arrested, charged with espionage, and hanged. It transpires that he and Juliet have been having a passionate love affair. In despair at the death of her lover she poisons herself. It is then revealed that Jemima, whose advances were spurned by Lawrence and who was crazed with jealousy, stole the personal possessions, and vengefully planted them in his cottage, together with material indicating that he was a German spy.

After the war Jemima writes a novel in memory of her sister and Lawrence, titling it *Restitution*. She then abandons writing and travels to Africa, where she spends the rest of her life helping out in a leper colony.

'It is as if George Eliot had never died,' *The Guardian* said admiringly. 'An instant classic' was the verdict of *Metro*'s Books of the Week. 'Forget Tolstoy,' advised florid, blotchy James Naughtie on the 'Today' programme. 'Forget every novelist who ever lived. We have Mick Owen. And believe me when I say that *Restitution* is the finest novel ever written.' In America they adored it. President Bush said it was a great book, really great (but refused to take questions).

President Bush. Now there was a guy... The Left, with wearisome predictability, wrote him off as a warmonger, a patron of extraordinary rendition, CIA dark sites, torture chambers in client states far from Oklahoma. Stuff and nonsense! George W was a genial fellow, with friendly twinkling eyes and a warm smile that was almost a chuckle. If he had a vice it was probably chemical (Mick, on a private visit to the White House, had once briefly spotted the President clapping a handful of pills to his mouth, in a slightly furtive manner). Mick was not a moralist: everyone was entitled to amphetamines, if they needed them. Plus they sometimes came with benefits. Look at Robert Lowell, for example.

What sheep the Left were, lining up to bleat about humanitarian interventions. The world needed policing and if it had to be done, who better to do it than genial, gum-chewing Yanks? They brought democracy, installed politicians of moderate views, and allowed business to flourish, showering benefits on the local population. Afghanistan, Iraq, Libya – the successes never ceased. There wasn't a lot left to sort out now, when you thought about it. Iran would need regime change, obviously. Ditto Russia. Syria also. There were in addition one or two states in Latin America that would probably need a visit from a coalition united under American leadership. After that, China. War was sometimes an unfortunate necessity, Mick felt. But the international rules-based order was a gem that must not be tarnished. Also in quite a few of those unruly places his books either sold badly or were not even stocked – after being brought into line these nations would undoubtedly benefit from the opening of hundreds of branches of Waterstones, bringing culture to aesthetically impoverished peoples.

But it was Laura who was the real fan. A charming and delightful woman. She rested her hand on his arm, looked him in the eyes (her own were, in truth, somewhat bloodshot) and purred that *Restitution* meant more to her than any novel she'd ever read. This was on the President's final state visit to his ally, Tone Blur. Laura's own soft intoxicating drawl was marinated in maple syrup, the Texan brand. This historic meeting took place inside Number Ten. Outside you could hear the chanting of the mob.[13] They were worked up about the invasion of Iraq and were roaring the usual wearisome and disagreeable slogans. Trust the Left to display impudence to an American President and his wife, who in fact had very refined literary tastes and were at the zenith of contemporary Texan cultural awareness!

Mick remembered how an official had entered the room and whispered that those noisy marchers were being diverted across Waterloo Bridge and along beside the station, returning

[13] 'the chanting of the mob': among its members that Thursday were David Cornwell, the actor Peter Capaldi, and the minor forgotten writer Elvis Blunt.

over Westminster Bridge. Mrs Bush and Mick should leave now for security reasons, before the rabble marched up Whitehall. Mick frowned and hurriedly finished his slice of Manhattan Délice Mousse. It really was appalling that a civilised conversation should be terminated in this way. One could not help but think of Mandelstam.

There were other movie adaptations of Mick's work, all memorialised in framed posters – moons to the two major planets. *Loving Lulu* (OK but it pulled its punches), *Berlin by Night* (a messy flop), *Endless Obsession* (suffered from hideous miscasting), *A Cheating Bitch* (gratuitous nudity and, to the dismay of cinemagoers, not about a dog at all) and *Final Act* (just about adequate, a bit flat really – and why that tweak of the original title?).

As you ascend you leave Hollywood behind and encounter art. Mick likes art, in a small way. See! There are the four Maggie Hambling oils he picked up at Snape – seascapes – cracking good value at 5K each. And up there, to the right, a small Lucien Freud canvas of a pig, alongside an early Hockney collage. All very sound investments.

Now nearly at the top.

11.46am The Landing

Taking three steps at a time Delphine crosses the final trio and reaches the landing.

On display here are some first editions and a selection of the innumerable translations. A kaleidoscope of coloured spines.

Plus more photographs of the author.

Here he is in attendance at many important conferences and cultural occasions. Here he is at some of his book launches, a champagne flute in one hand, discoursing. Here he is seen on a platform, at a lectern.

Look! An intimate image captures him curled up on a large sofa, book in hand. And there he is again, again at a table with Christopher Hitchens. Two wine bottles are in attendance. Plus there are clusters of pictures of him with other novelists. In Sydney with Peter Carey. In Biarritz with Julian Barnes. In Brooklyn Heights, with someone unidentifiable. (A whisper in your ear. That's Tom Pynchon, bearded, wearing Ray-Bans.)

More of Mart. A handsome devil in those early images, long hair brushing against his collar. Later, sour-mouthed, his hair receded like the coast at Happisburgh, his furrowed face perpetually marinated in vinegar. Angry about unsympathetic Arabs; furious with the futility and follies of the Left.

Smiling Salman, against the background of a large lawn with a big spreading cedar at the far end. Salman, in his heroic period, bodyguards somewhere nearby, just outside the frame. Salman, rich with self-satisfaction, in not the slightest doubt who is much the greater genius present in this pairing. His stomach, his waistline, expands a little each year. But the fat will not protect him from the horror that awaits him, further down the corridor of the years. When it occurs, Mick will feel a certain satisfaction at the confirmation of his granite opinions where Islam is concerned – and that ghastly crew of Leftists who associate with it. Iran, Mick is in no doubt, must be dealt with. He is with the Israelis on that.

Famous chums – the cream of the intelligentsia and the finest novelists in the world! He knows them all.

That small beaming figure with the neatly trimmed beard. Is that Harvard in the background? And another one of the two of them together: unquestionably Oxford.

Tim. Good old Tim. You could always rely on him to steady the ship when the going gets rough. *The Guardian* was always there with its platform. It made the paper still well worth buying, despite its anorexia.

In today's paper: Timothy Garton-Ash and why we should take out Moscow before it's too late.

In today's paper: Timothy Garton-Ash and why we need to go to war with China – before it's too late.

You could always rely on Tim to see the bigger picture.

Look!

Here's Mick with David Cornwell, in a London park on a dull, dark day, both men wearing winter coats. He sought his advice for *Castor Oil*, his novel about a woman spy. The book had not been a success.

It was a painful shock after the great man's death to discover that the published edition of his letters included one in which he described *Restitution* as 'a sugar-coated turd'. No matter. Cornwell's reputation would never recover from Suleika Dawson's devastating sex memoir.

On she runs, Delphine, and on they go beside her, the bookshelves. They occupy all the wall space to a height of two metres. On one of the bottom shelves, at ankle height, next to a book on archetypes by Northrop Frye,[14] is a wrinkled white spine with the title *The Well Wrought Urn* in black and the author's name, Cleanth Brooks, in brown.

Cleanth? (Don't frown – he's an American.)

Plus 'UP' – for University Paperbacks – and the volume

[14] 'Northrop Frye': a fashionable literary theorist in the late 1960s and early 1970s. A Canadian. What person of intelligence and understanding could not but be impressed by his sparkling observation that 'Even the human heart is slightly left of centre', although the emphasis of every snivelling bourgeois liberal capitalist-imperialist collaborator is inevitably on the *slightly*.

number: 185. Inside is an autograph of the owner:[15] *Dippy Scott*. Remove this book from its cramped and obscure location and flip it over. On the back there's a helpful description of its contents. The book's essential argument is that 'poetry depends primarily for its total realisation upon a concentrated and sympathetic reading of the text'.

Eh? Isn't that a statement of the bleedin' obvious?

The author discusses ten texts in particular. The jacket supplies a list of them. John Donne's 'The Canonization'. Shakespeare's *Macbeth*. (Eh? That's a play, not a poem!) Milton's 'L'Allegro' and 'Il Penseroso'. John Herrick's 'Corinna's Going a-Maying'. Alexander Pope's *The Rape of the Lock*. Thomas Gray's 'Elegy written in a Country Churchyard'. Keats's 'Ode on a Grecian Urn'. Tennyson's 'Tears, Idle Tears'. Yeats's 'Among School Children'.

Open the book at any angle and you discover that Cleanth is fussily correcting imaginary readers who torment his sense of what's true. There's a crowd of readers beating against the door to his study – an army of wild-eyed zombies who are driven by the feeling that great poetry can be 'free from any of the glozings of rhetoric'.

Glozings? WTF?

To gloze is to gloss – to offer a commentary or an explanation. And without explainers – priests – academic critics – newsreaders – opinion columnists – where would we be? Sweating with anxious ignorance. Priests, academic critics, newsreaders, opinion columnists – they know we need them to set out the facts and to interpret them.

Cleanth insists that no matter is intrinsically poetic. What must be sniffed out, as a truffle hog goes to it, nosing out a fruity delicious subterranean fungus, is *the poet's imaginative grasp, intricate and complex*, yielding many critical paragraphs.

[15] 'the owner': This volume is now in the library of Ellis Sharp. Quite by what route it came to arrive there is, at the time of writing, unknown. Research on this matter continues. (F. D.)

*

Dippy was doing Eng Lit. She arrived in Norwich at the same time as Mick and Gwynedd. And when she rocked up at Alan Burns's seminar for creatives – all welcome – she scanned the room. Her eyes met Mick's. It was a consummation just like the one in Thomas Hardy's *Titanic* poem. Somewhere in an upstairs room the Spinner of the Years had been working hard on the plot. In the summer of that year no mortal eye could have seen the intimate welding of Dippy and Mick's histories, although it would not be many more weeks before Mick was spending less and less time with Gwynedd in the flat on Unthank Road and more and more time at UEA.

Davinia Scott, known to her family and friends as Dippy. A nickname acquired in early childhood (ice-cream tub, hand, the relentless satisfaction of appetite). Wordsworth's famous thesis that the child is mother to the woman proved true in later life. Fellatio was her favourite flavour.

At first sight Dippy looked much like many other female students of that era. She was tall, slender, her jet-black hair dropped as far as the base of her spine. She favoured floral dresses that extended from her throat to her ankles. The flowers were white daisies, sprinkled across a chocolate background. Good enough to eat...

It was the time when, should you be travelling to San Francisco on a business trip, you had to be sure to wear some flowers in your hair. Money was never referred to as money but as 'bread' (except in the bakery where Gwynedd worked). Men talking to other men punctuated every sentence with 'man'. *Easy Rider* was the bestest movie ever made.[16]

[16] '*Easy Rider* was the bestest movie ever made': It's easy enough now to laugh at some of this movie's risible dialogue and contradictions. Turning your back on the modern world by stamping on your watch and then riding off on a large motorbike – as fatuous gestures go that takes some beating. The ethos of dropping out, man, playing it cool, man, doing your own thing, man, can only ever be comfortably accomplished with the backing of a parental tax-deductible Trust Fund and a pleasant swathe of rural acres. That said, the last ten

Dippy wanted to appear normal, like all the other rich, posh girls who came to UEA in 1970. But she had a terrible secret. Not even her closest female friend knew of the horror in her background. The disgusting reality was that her father was a Conservative MP.

Luckily for her Scott was a not particularly unusual surname. If the name brought anything to mind it was Scott of the Antarctic or his son Peter Scott, famous for his wildlife conservation and banal watercolours of ducks in flight.

Dippy's branch of the family was entirely unrelated to those Scotts. Her father Alexander Scott was a war hero and not remotely interested in birds – at least not the feathered sort. His constituency was a large seaside town on the south coast, a place he detested. He was one of those MPs you've never heard of until they become enmeshed in scandal. A wizened, small man, he bore a distinct resemblance to Lord Beaverbrook (making a display of adjectives quite unnecessary).

Dippy wore an African bead necklace and displayed a copper bangle on her wrists to ward off bad vibrations. She had high cheekbones and the eyes of Cleopatra.[17] Her taste in fiction was lamentably fashionable – the Penguins of stodgy, solemn, humourless Herman Hesse, Leonard Cohen's slick empty *Beautiful Losers*, Jack Kerouac's wearisome hipster picaresque which gushed through lustreless prose, the sugary Californian cuteness of fatuous Richard Brautigan. Dippy had high regard

minutes of the movie are as good as anything cinema has ever produced in the way of endings. In this respect it can sit comfortably alongside *The Third Man*, *The Wild Bunch* and *Człowiek z żelaza*. Nor let us forget Jack Nicholson's heartfelt tribute to a remarkable English novelist – even though those remarks may, in the twenty-first century, appear to be acutely uncomplimentary.

[17] 'the eyes of Cleopatra': A nonsensical description since no detailed evidence of Cleopatra's real appearance survives. The colour of her eyes and hair are as unknown and contested as that of her skin. In so far as the description means anything it is probably an allusion to the rather fetching shade of purple eyeliner which Dippy used in those days.

for Cohen's doggerel (unforgettably squashed by Jonathan Raban in *The Society of the Poem* as equivalent to 'the confections of a Sinatra'). Her dubious taste in novels and verse was matched by her fondness for astrology, alternative medicine and flying saucers.

Dippy tinkled as she drifted through the days, like a wind chime. Her copper rings held back a multiplicity of bad vibes; crystals on slender silver chains combated innumerable ailments by radiating healing rays; remedies derived from the heavily diluted juice of crushed dandelions and various herbs were contained in miniature glass bottles, hung on leather cords from her belt. She went nowhere without her little box of I Ching sticks. In her presence there was much chatter about Yin and Yang, cosmic balance, and ancient wisdom from parts of India still lacking modern sanitation. It was her strong belief that the Shroud of Turin proved that Jesus survived the crucifixion. He subsequently made his way to India, where in his younger days (a bit like Shakespeare's 'lost years') he had studied Buddhism. Dippy was convinced that the German theologian Kersten was correct in his belief that Jesus lived to a ripe old age and was buried in a tomb in Kashmir which still exists to this day, shamefully neglected by his global fan base.[18] Before a journey Dippy always consulted her Tarot pack.

It was perhaps no surprise that after her acrimonious divorce she wrote two books[19] which only served to confirm the strong

[18] See Holger Kersten, *Jesus lived in India*, with 57 illustrations (partially coloured), Shaftesbury, Dorset: Element Books, 1991.

[19] 'two books': Davinia Scott, *The Soul and the Cosmos* (1997) and *Psychospiritual Teachings of Ancient Times* (1999) – both published by The Bliss Press, East Eden, California. Even though they were written and published after their divorce, it is the melancholy task of any biographer of Mick Owen to read these two execrable texts for the light they shed on her personality and her fictional reincarnation as the wife in *Woman with a Cat*. They confirm that that work's acid description of 'Lavinia' as possessing 'a mind as narrow as her waist and as cloudy as the summit of a Scottish mountain in November' was, in truth, a reasonable one. *The Soul and the Cosmos* drew on Tibetan

suspicion that Mick's *Woman with a Cat* was a blistering satire on a wife with weird notions, who with the assistance of a very expensive lawyer he would shortly set free in the brisk manner of a vet administering an injection to an ailing pet. *Woman with a Cat*, reviewers, said, was plainly influenced by *The Witches of Eastwick* – but in a good way.

The novel is about a brilliant evolutionary biologist, Dick Ewing, whose life suffers a series of mysterious setbacks, the source only becoming clear when the household cat is injured by a passing car, resulting in his wife becoming ill. The strange connections between the cat and the wife become increasingly clear, leading to the startling revelation that the wife is a witch, that her meat stews are devilish in conception and that she

Tantricism in its guide to personal enlightenment via such misty routes as the Path of Liberation and the Tangible Path. These involve much abstract, windy rhetoric about the identity of energy and consciousness, the sharpening of the mind through the use of Energy Yoga, breathing exercises and, in the highest state of meditation, the transformation of the body's circulatory system, fluids and secretions. Its sequel, *Psychospiritual Teachings of Ancient Times*, derived from the same sources to develop its tips about the twelve indispensable things in life – a guru, special instruction, intellect, an aversion to the material world, invulnerability to temptation, purity of mind, willingness to embrace the whole of knowledge, the appropriate system of meditation, the devotion of body, speech and mind to the True Path, a suitable methodology for implementing the True Teachings, the acquisition of knowledge to avoid pitfalls, dangers and misleading paths, faith and serenity at the moment of death, and the achievement of spiritual powers capable of bodily transformation. Those who manage to acquire these twelve indispensable things are, the book asserted, in a strong position to transmute quicksilver into almost the same amount of gold, better than ordinary gold in that it is softer and more malleable – as was conclusively accomplished by Nicolas Flamel on 25 April 1382, at five o'clock in the evening, in the presence of an unimpeachable witness, his wife Perrenelle. Davinia Scott, alas, does not seem to have reached this final state of enlightenment and was last heard of managing a bar in Frome, Somerset.

plans to sacrifice Dick at the next full moon.

But in the great conflict between scientific rationality and witchcraft, science comes out on top, rhetorically. Meteorology supplies the final triumph as Lavinia is struck by a bolt of lightning at the very moment she holds a knife high to plunge it into the bare chest of her bound husband. Lavinia's heart explodes, her body blazes, and the flames scorch the ropes which bind the long-suffering husband, allowing him to break free.

In a charming final last chapter, set one year later, Dick Ewing is shown happily married to an attractive and much younger colleague and living a new life in a rose-bordered cottage in Suffolk, while blackbirds chirp and collar doves coo.

One sour critic called *Woman with a Cat* 'sexist trash, diluted gothic garbage, and sugary kitsch of the highest order' but the rest were in agreement that this was another masterpiece by a novelist of extraordinary talent.

But all this happened some two decades after he first met Dippy. In those early days Mick found her simply adorable. She lived up to her nickname: she was dreamy, spaced out, easy-going. Plus she was an enthusiastic gobbler – quite unusual for English girls in those days. Consumed by desire Mick happily overlooked her deplorable literary judgements and her crackpot beliefs.

This latter aspect of her character derived entirely from her father. After his divorce from Gwynedd, Mick got to know Alexander Scott very well. He liked the MP enormously. The fellow wasn't a snob. He may have owned a castle but he raised no objection to his darling daughter marrying a chap from the lower middle class. He said he'd read In *Bed with Emily* and *Loving Lulu* and thought they were 'splendid' and 'delightful'.

Alexander was not a moralist. Apart from his castle in Wales his possessions included a wife, Laura, an invalid, who never left their mews home in Kensington, and a P.A., Betsy, who accompanied him everywhere, except the marital bed in London. (Alexander did not believe that Laura would be up for a threesome, so never attempted even the most tentative of enquiries.)

Betsy – known to friends and family as 'big Betsy' or 'bouncing Betsy' – had ginger hair, freckles everywhere (arms, face, breasts, sprinkled over her spine, even across the twin hillsides of her impressive rump). She was posh, hearty, thirtyish. Plump but not fat. She bounced when she moved. She did not wear a bra.

Bouncing Betty's breasts were as restless as two plums on a plum tree in a gale. She was a touchy-feely gal, whose hands were always dropping down to rest on nearby knees and forearms. Her cheeks were rosy as the finest specimen of Cox's apple. Everyone loved Betsy. She was as bubbly and innocent as a puppy. To be with Betsy was like being beside a roaring log fire in a cottage on a hillside in a blizzard. The snow out there lies two feet deep, the other rooms in the property are cold as ice, but no matter – to be with Betty is to feel her warmth, rippling over you in waves. Betty's eyes always twinkle. Her smile shimmers. She's a gal who rarely says no to anything.

The whole castle knew when she orgasmed, for she bellowed like a bull. Glassware trembled on shelves. Usually, as she came, her sphincter loosened and a litre or so of intestinal gas squirted free with a noise very reminiscent of six trumpeters practising for an important royal occasion. Nobody minded the faintly lingering gassy aftermath. It sweetened the building's cold and somewhat musty corridors. But not even Betty's glowing and fragrant presence could combat the slowly spreading damp.

Alexander Scott's chief interest in life, after sex, was the Warminster mystery. Skywatching! Skywatchers! Things took off, so to speak, in 1964 – and continued for a decade. Warminster in Wiltshire – a small town on the edge of Salisbury Plain, where some residents began hearing mysterious sounds. A strange humming. What sounded like giant hailstones clattering on the roof. A crash as if a giant chimney-stack had been wrenched from a roof and scattered in pieces. Aeronautical amblings of a Thing in malevolent mood! A gigantic tin can with huge nuts and bolts inside it, rattling in the sky! And then aural mysteries transformed into visual ones.

Hilda Hebdidge saw unusual objects in the sky. They were cigar-shaped and covered in winking lights. Kathleen Penton saw a shining Thing gently moving in the sky, with windows similar to portholes. She said it resembled a train carriage, gliding sideways. Rachel Atwil was woken by a droning noise which made her bed shake. Looking out of the window, she saw a bright object like a massive star, huge in size, and definitely domed on top.

It was plainly necessary that this matter be investigated. When the war ended Alexander Scott DSC had become bored. He'd had a good war, packed with adventure (tank battles in Libya, capture by the Italians, escape from a POW camp, recapture by the Germans, a leap from a train while under armed guard, escape across occupied Europe to Switzerland). Marriage and fatherhood was a rite of passage he found dreary. Becoming an MP seemed thrilling at first – membership of the finest gentleman's club in the land. But he soon grew bored with Parliamentary business and the division bell. He lacked ambition. He had no wish to become Prime Minister or Foreign Secretary. He was a party loyalist, whose vote could always be relied upon. His views were always shaped by those of his party.

His route to excitement, beyond those supplied by Betsy and her predecessors, began with a subscription to *Flying Saucer Review*. He became something of an expert in the field. His status as a war hero and an MP made him a very welcome member of this fringe fraternity. Alexander Scott supplied lunacy with a crust of respectability. He was delighted to accept the invitation to become Director of The Warminster Extraordinary Phenomena Team (WEPT), a ragtag assemblage of West Country hippies, excitable military veterans, thirty-something divorcees looking for love, and miscellaneous addicts of the paranormal united only by their lack of interest in science and sociology. WEPT was affiliated to BUFORA (the British UFO Research Association) and OLLM (the Organisation of Ley-Line Mappers).

WEPT had an office in town in a one-room flat above a

betting shop, and a pair of khaki caravans parked at Cradle Hill, the perfect UFO-spotting site, just north of the town. The hill was widely acknowledged to be a cosmic energy centre, constantly recharged from its proximity to the hill-fort at Battlesbury and the tumulus of Copheap, and beyond them long barrows, round barrows, circle after circle rippling outward as far as Glastonbury, Stonehenge and Avebury.

Mick spent several uncomfortable weekends in those caravans, humouring Dippy as she searched the night sky for alien visitors.[20] Three times they saw strange lights moving

[20] 'several uncomfortable weekends': The novelist's discomforts were mild in comparison with others of his age, and older, who worked on building sites at this time. Conditions were dangerous, pay was poor, sanitation was often rudimentary, labour was zero contract. In September 1972, while WEPT members scrutinised the sky for extra-terrestrials, six coaches took trades union activists to picket large building sites in the Shrewsbury area. The aim was to encourage exploited and badly treated site workers to join a union. The event passed off peacefully, with police present and no arrests. Five months later, entirely unexpectedly, twenty-four of the pickets were arrested and charged with more than 240 offences between them. The first trials resulted in acquittals or minor convictions. But fresh trials in Shrewsbury involved the six trade unionists regarded as the leaders being charged under an 1875 Act with 'conspiracy to intimidate contrary to common law'. This ancient law had never previously been used in an industrial dispute. It was a blatantly political prosecution inspired by the major building firms with the collusion of the corrupt and reactionary Tory Home Secretary, Robert Carr, the police, the Crown Prosecution Service and the capitalist judiciary. The motivation was to protect the profits and dangerous working practices of the employers and deter trade union activism. The day after the prosecution closed its case Independent Television broadcast a highly prejudicial documentary about the case, *Red under the Bed*, which was plainly designed to influence the jury. (A more modern instance of blatant political interference by the depraved and poisonously reactionary corporate media is BBC TV's tendentious 'Panorama' documentary on alleged anti-Semitism within the Labour Party, broadcast just before the 2019 general election.) It must be

silently across the heavens which, mercifully, proved sufficient excitement for her.

After that he coaxed her into a preference for a cottage in the hills outside Nice, bought with the advance on a three-novel deal cooked up for him by his super-powered agent. The dinner party scene in *Woman with a Cat* in which Dick coolly denounces 'New Age morons beside Salisbury Plain, converting military manoeuvres into extraterrestrial oddities' is plainly rooted in that idyllic early phase of his relationship with Dippy.[21] But one can have too much of Dippy and her father.

remembered that in those days there were only two television broadcasters: the BBC and ITV. Independent Television (an oxymoron) broadcast *Red under the Bed* across ITV regions on 13 November 1973, the day after the prosecution closed its case. We know that the judge watched it and it is inconceivable that the jury didn't. Plainly it influenced their guilty verdicts. The programme was fronted by Woodrow Wyatt, who as you might expect from a disgusting lackey of the capitalist state, was a former Labour MP. The documentary even included footage of Shrewsbury Crown Court. The programme makers were supplied with information by the so-called Information Research Department – the outfit that the stool pigeon George Orwell supplied his list of Reds to. The Department of Employment, MI5 and the Prime Minister Edward Heath were also involved. It was a conspiracy to pervert the course of justice involving all the agencies of the capitalist state. The TV programme sought to suggest that the trades unionists were Communist subversives who used violence against peaceful workers and sought to overthrow the state. These blatantly prejudicial libels worked. Found guilty, those identified as the ringleaders were sent to prison – for the crime of seeking to improve working practices and pay. The corruption of British policing, the judicial system, and the corporate media was never more blatantly exposed than here. The full, ugly story was uncovered not by a journalist but by a single determined amateur and later turned into a book: Eileen Turnbull, *A Very British Conspiracy – The Shrewsbury 24 and the Campaign for Justice* (London: Verso Books, 2022).

[21] 'military manoeuvres': Owen takes refuge in vagueness; a better writer, absorbing Nabokov's insistence on concrete, sharply observed

Suffice it to say that after several years of happy marriage the relationship soured. Mick inadvertently discovered that some of his closest friends privately called her 'Drippy'. And then, one ordinary grey day, subsequently resonant with fate of the very highest order, he met Delphine. She was in television and her company was making a documentary about him. Light drizzle put a sparkle in her hair and hung a tiny bell from each of her lobes. A slight tinkling as of a wind chime lightly brushed by a gust across his heart soon turned into a pianoforte rhapsody. It was followed by a complete orchestra and massive choir engaged with Mahler at his most full-blooded and passionate. Delphine spoke English in a husky sensuous accent; her eyes shone, her smile was natural, she was Parisian, highly educated, was intimate with every volume by Proust, had a place in Deauville. Inhaling her perfume, Mick felt dizzy, intoxicated, alive. Dippy's dreary delusions abruptly lost what little was left of their charm; Delphine's sophisticated tastes supplanted them. Before long, divorce proceedings were set in motion.

It was a shock when Dippy refused to do the decent thing and go quietly. Things became acrimonious, then hellish. Mick envied T. S. Eliot and the good old days. In that glorious era all you required was an understanding doctor. If anyone needed despatching to the padded cells, straitjackets, and long cold corridors of a lunatic asylum, he felt very strongly, very bitterly, it was Dippy. Alas, those kinds of doctor no longer existed, or if they did they were powerless. Fortunately one could still rely on the London judiciary to stand up for a multi-millionaire when the going got rough, tough and more than enough. *The Fifth Act* was Mick's thank you letter to them – a short novel about a group of High Court judges and other legal professionals involved in amateur dramatics. During a production of *Hamlet* two of the cast are murdered. The killer

detail and accuracy of observation, would have made reference to orange flares, the scarlet passage of tracer shells, low flying helicopters and other aircraft, as well as searchlights which, under the right conditions, can appear along the underside of clouds as brightly lit moving ellipsoid objects.

turns out to be Davina Wales, a deranged woman consumed by bitterness about the judge's verdict in her divorce proceedings. 'Blackly comic,' the critics said – Davina bungles her revenge and kills two judges who were not involved in her case. After being shot by a police marksman she has her life saved by the very judge who found in her husband's favour. 'Dazzling,' said the *Guardian*.

From the generously wide landing a narrower set of stairs rises from the eastern end, disappearing into a large rectangular hatchway cut in the ceiling. It dates back to when the loft was converted in 1957.

Delphine sprints up the soft carpeted steps and emerges into what was once the old roof space.

11.46am The Loft

The old conversion to full width dormers on both sides, each with a gable roof, was upgraded when Mick bought Kipling Manor. A corridor filled with sunlight runs between the rooms on either side. This top floor of the house is strictly Mick and Delphine's private space. Guests are not encouraged to wander here. On the west side is the gym – a place of mirrored walls and gleaming equipment. An exercise bike set before a screen big enough to watch movies on. A running belt. A rowing-machine. Weights. A pair of wrist-thick ropes which descend from the ceiling. Rings for hanging from. Bars along one wall, suitable for climbing. All the latest devices for keeping the human body trim and in reasonable shape. In an adjacent room a Jacuzzi. Next to that the sauna. All easily accessed from their gigantic bedroom, which is flanked on one side by a dressing room bigger than the average British lounge and on the other by their open plan en-suite bathrooms – his and hers, with separate lavatories. Each basin bears a matching soapstone pot from Ishkar. They share the enormous bath. As for that bedroom. Note the Vispring bed with the Baronet mattress and the table by Alvar Aalto. Reflect on sheer good taste in the heritage looking glass. Note the Yves Saint Laurent Rouge Sur Mesure lipstick maker. Note the exquisite plants, so perfect they might almost be plastic. But they are not. They had the team from Jam Jar in to give them that muted yet insistent green ambience that the bedroom seemed to require. Before departing, acknowledge the surprisingly comfortable ruby-coloured Ouverture sofa by Pierluigi Cerri. That was Delphine's choice. Mick prefers to rest his increasingly wrinkled bottom on his rare How High the Moon chair by Shiro Kramata.

And still Mick is screaming, though the screams seem more irregular now, perhaps even a little less loud. It is like that moment when a washing machine, having reached maximum velocity on Full Spin, diminishes a little in volume and begins to slow down, like a panting septuagenarian on a long rural walk.

*

Violence.

Mick's first taste of it was when he was at primary school in Shoreham-By-Sea. A Friday, May 11, 1956. The time was a quarter past one and it was the lunch break. He was playing marbles near the toilet block. Everyone saw the aircraft, though none could have said what it was.[22] They watched in awe as the immense, low-flying bomber passed overhead. And then it happened. The noise of the engines suddenly faded. The aircraft flew on in silence, then banked. Someone on board ejected, shooting across the sky. A parachute blossomed, then almost at once dropped out of sight with its swaying cargo.

Mick's fist tightened around his marble. With everyone else in the playground he stared, enthralled, as the bomber dipped, then abruptly plummeted to earth. It vanished behind a row of houses and the high brick wall around the playground. Next there was the piercing, reverberating sound of a terrific explosion. A moment later a pillar of black oily smoke surged upward, perhaps a mile away, expanding as it rose.

To everyone's fury a teacher herded them inside.

It was only later, when he was home, that the great adventure began. Mick's father in those days was working at Shoreham airport. He was in a hangar at the time and had not witnessed the crash. When he came home at the end of the day he was keen to visit the crash site, and took Mick with him.

Although he never wrote about it, and told only two people about it – Delphine and Sam Quiggly – Mick never forgot that day. The crash site was only a short walk from their house on Kingston Lane.[23] They approached it down a residential street still littered with wreckage. In those days there were no

[22] 'what it was': Valiant B1 WP202 of the Royal Aircraft Establishment. The Vickers-Armstrongs Valiant was a British four-jet bomber, capable of carrying atom bombs. This particular aircraft was on an equipment test flight from Farnborough Airport. When the equipment failed to work it was decided to burn off fuel before returning. The pilot therefore flew along the south coast at a low altitude.

[23] 'their house on Kingston Lane': Number 40.

cordons or police guards. The public could wander freely among the ruins. Only the recreation ground where the main body of the bomber lay was closed.

What Mick remembered most of all was the sight of semi-detached houses with their roof tiles ripped off, blown away by the force of the blast as the aircraft exploded. The wooden beams lay exposed like the bones of a dead animal whose carcase has been hollowed out by predators. The street was littered with dark blackened debris. He walked with his father as far as the recreation ground entrance, where a small crowd had gathered. Afterwards they retraced their steps through aircraft wreckage and returned home. Life went on.

It wasn't until the arrival of the internet and the onset of old age that Mick went back into his past and found out what happened that day. It seemed that the plane's electrics had suddenly failed, making it impossible to control. Suspicion fell on the civilian engineer, Alan Knight. It was theorized that he may have been resetting the circuit breakers on the test equipment, thereby causing the malfunction. Three of the four men on board died in the crash: Knight, the pilot, Kenneth Orman, 33, and the navigator, Kenneth Evans, also 33. The co-pilot, Colin Preece, successfully ejected, though he was injured when, still attached to the seat, he crashed down onto the ticket office at Southwick station.

Twenty-five years separated the future novelist from the dead pilot and the dead navigator. Their faceless ghosts followed him down the years. On his fiftieth birthday they would have been seventy-five. When he became seventy-five they might still have been alive, shrivelled and liver-spotted, dozing in a sunlit armchair in a retirement home, in a lounge smelling of floor polish.

The thought of it made him reach for his treasured green bottle of Laphroaig.

Violence.

On that May day in 1956 Mick Owen was just a child. He knew nothing of British history, apart from the banal scraps served up at his Shoreham-by-Sea primary school. Prehistoric man (keen on fur shorts and hairy capes). The Romans (gave us tiled floors and their soldiers wore pleated leather skirts). 1066 (an arrow hit the king in the eye, which is why everyone should be extra careful during archery lessons). The Armada (God, who is in charge of the weather, is definitely pro-British). Oliver Cromwell (wore a tin helmet and tried to stop the royal family; he failed). The British Empire (did its best to help people around the world, even though some of them were very bad people, who put English people in a nasty black hole in Calcutta, which is in India).

Three years earlier, on his first day at school, Mick Owen wept. He missed his mummy. There were no pre-school nurseries in those days. You spent your first five years with your mother. The highlight of the day was when she turned the wireless on and the two of you tuned into 'Listen with Mother'. Mick still had a vivid Proustian memory of the signature tune, the warmth of his mother's presence, the faint aroma of floor polish. Mother kept the house tidy and highly polished, did the washing with museum devices including a wooden roller for squeezing out the water from sodden clothes, bought the groceries, and had a meal on the table when father came home from work. She baked ceaselessly – biscuits and cakes. She let him lick the bowl after the mix had been transferred to trays. Decades later he gorged on Ben & Jerry's Cookie Dough, addicted to the sensual satisfactions of his old four-year-old self. Once mother inadvertently set fire to the kitchen curtains. He still remembered the brief pillar of fire, and then the flakes of burnt fabric. Mother adored her little Michael, her only child, her special darling.

To be wrenched from this idyll and led to a bus stop and put on an omnibus and waved bye-bye was an abomination. He sobbed with shock. He wept ceaselessly. To cheer him up his class teacher let him pull a milk crate down the corridor. How it clattered and crashed and made a scrumptious scraping noise! Those were the days. A third of a pint of milk every day, for every schoolchild. That delicious inch of cream at the top.

Taken away by the Tories. *Margaret Thatcher, milk snatcher!*

But best of all was Empire Day, 1953. Mick was still melancholy at his motherless school days. To pep him up it was agreed that he should lead the entire school around the playground with the big school Union Jack. Every other child had a small flag, and the staff had medium-size flags. He held the Big One. How his heart swelled with pride. *Thump! Thump! Thump!* Round and round they went in circles, waving their red, white and blue flags.[24] The British Empire – he had no idea what it was but he was proud and excited to be celebrating it.

But that was the last year it was celebrated. This glorious day was quietly shelved. The Empire was undergoing a period of adjustment. A wind of change was blowing through the colonies. Instead of being run by a degenerate white elite it was becoming necessary to replace them with a degenerate black elite. 'Independence'. Of course one or two of these blighters took the word at face value and even believed they should run matters for the benefit of their own people! Pure Bolshevism. One cannot let essentially backward people run mines and oil refineries.

Yes, foreign policy was quietly, remotely going about its murderous business far beyond the blue horizon while Mick paddled his tootsies on Shoreham beach that long hot August. In faraway Iran – on the very edge of the school curriculum – geography – atlases – 'the Middle East' – coloured countries in every sense – Persia it was called in the older editions – faraway unimaginable places – here it was that the country's first democratically elected government, under its popular leader Mohammad Mosaddegh, nationalised the Anglo-Iranian Oil Company (now known as BP – British Petroleum). BP was effectively looting the country of its prime material resource

[24] 'red, white and blue': highly appropriate colours – red for the ocean of blood shed by this atrocity-loaded repressive Empire, blue for the foul-smelling swamp of conservative 'values' which supplied its ideology, white for the erasure of this history from the consciousness of the average British citizen.

and revenue stream. The old, old story. Mohammad Mosaddegh wished to return that wealth to the people of Iran. But within days of the nationalisation (May 1951) the Labour government of the degenerate blood-soaked imperialist Clement Attlee set in motion the mechanics of a coup d'état. When at the next election the Conservatives took over they continued the organisation of the overthrow of an elected government and its leader. They identified a suitable military leader, the previously pro-Nazi General Fazlollah Zahedi. A good chap. Malleable. British embassy official Sam Falle met him on 6 August. It was arranged that after the coup he would become Prime Minister.

Meanwhile MI6 and a Foreign Office team met with the CIA. British bribes brought on board senior army officers, newspaper editors, street thugs and others, to implement the coup. That murderous racist Winston Churchill was itching for action. CIA thug Kermit Roosevelt Junior met the playboy Shah, Mohammad Reza Pahlavi. *The plot was orchestrated with the assistance of the BBC, which agreed to send the signal for the coup to start.* **HOW MANY PEOPLE KNOW THAT?**

The BBC's Persian language news broadcast began on the agreed date not with the usual 'it is now midnight in London' but with 'it is now exactly midnight'. The green light from London! The Shah left the country, leaving behind signed blank decrees dismissing Mosaddegh and replacing him with General Zahedi, while street demonstrations funded by the CIA and MI6 broke out. Three-hundred people died in the coup. Under the Shah political dissent was suppressed, torture chambers were established, and some 10,000 people died. In 1975 Amnesty International said that Iran had 'the highest rate of death penalties in the world, no valid system of civilian courts and a history of torture which is beyond belief'. All thanks to Clement Attlee, the BBC, MI6, the CIA, Winston Churchill and many others. And let us not forget Norman Darbyshire, a British intelligence officer who was at the centre of orchestrating this very British coup and who was personally involved in the murder of Mahmoud Afshartous, the Iranian chief of police, who was deemed to be too loyal to the elected government and its leader.

Don't expect to hear about this anytime soon on that state propaganda sewer, the BBC.[25]

Violence.

It had punctuated Mick's years in London. There were the IRA bombings of the 1970s. There were occasional cordons as streets were blocked off because of suspicious vehicles or objects. There had been some cancellations of concerts because of bomb threats. Several times he was at an event when everyone was hurried out of the building. More tangibly, he had a dim memory of shattered glass near Piccadilly – the residue of an explosion the night before. Twice he heard bombs explode. One was the Baltic Exchange bomb, the other the Bishopsgate tipper truck bomb a year later. Both were extraordinarily loud. They'd seemed terrifyingly close.

And then there were the riots of 2011. Mick never forgot that awful day he jetted into Gatwick from Atlanta after attending a conference on the novel. He had been too busy Stateside to pay much attention to the news. A taxi took him into town. On the road to the Blackwall Tunnel there was a sudden view of the capital's skyline. Pillars of black oily smoke were rising from half a dozen widely spread locations. It looked like an old Second World War photograph, taken the morning after a Luftwaffe raid. Mick distinctly remembered saying to the cab driver (a taciturn Asiatic) 'What is going *on*?' But never ask a taxi driver for information. You will receive a monologue which goes on far too long.

That had been an unnerving time. Law and order seemed to

[25] It is obvious that this sentence and certain preceding paragraphs could not have possibly have been written by Sam Quiggly, as no American – least of all a Californian pothead – would write in this overwrought fashion. Wait for the final twist, *mes amis*, when, in the finest tradition of contemporary genre-based LitFic, everything becomes clear!

have completely broken down. It made Mick shiver. The trouble seemed to be restricted to cities. But one never knew when rioters might develop the thought that out there in the countryside were big houses, full of valuable stuff, occupied by tiny handfuls of individuals. The thought accelerated Mick's interest in taking shooting lessons and acquiring a small armoury. Tomorrow never knows...

Down the sunlight flooded corridor Delphine runs, to the staircase at the far end.

She pays no attention to the posters which line the corridor's length. In bright colours they testify to old art shows and RSC performances she and her famous husband had graced with their presence. The inevitable Picasso. Matisse. Various Impr-essionists. Stanley Spencer. A white fencing mask (Jonathan Slinger's *Hamlet*). Slinger's unforgettable *Richard III.*

Slinger's *Macbeth*, which was unforgettable in another way – the reopened refurbished theatre's smoke machine triggered fire alarms across the auditorium. Out they went, to stand in the crowd outside. Mick immediately attracting fans. He was charming as always. His fountain pen was ready for action. He thrilled them with his autograph. Something to pass on to the grandchildren.

'A marvellous performance,' someone said, and at first Mick thought that in some sophisticated and oblique way they were talking about his latest masterpiece. But as this personage (who does not deserve further mention in a biography devoted to genius) continued, praising Slinger, Mick quickly swallowed the word 'Thanks' and corrected himself, all smiles. 'Yes, marvellous,' he agreed. But his smile at that fleeting instant of his long and distinguished life seemed a little forced and frosty.

And then the emergency was over and they were invited back inside.

11.47am The Tower

As she reaches the foot of the stylish circular scarlet staircase that rises from the attic room floor to the hole cut in the roof, she tears off her sandals. Her bare feet – her toes – will get a better grip on the steps. She doesn't want to slip. Her soles meet the cold metal steps. Hurriedly, she ascends, her firm petite breasts flopping just a little. Her palms barely touch the slender curling banister. Her feet shed the last of the chlorine-scented droplets still clinging to her skin.

At the top, through the hole, you move off the final step into a small plain hallway, barely big enough to accommodate two people. It faces the door which opens into Mick's den. It has a lock but the novelist never uses it, except when he is away from home. Delphine knows better than to disturb him here when he is at work. It is, quite literally, his room at the top. A novel which he regards very highly and occasionally mentions in interviews. Poor John Braine. Success destroyed him. He moved away from his creative roots in the north and settled in the south, among stockbrokers and golf-club bores. Like Lawrence before him, the talented working-class lad slithered ineluctably to the Right. His *Weltanschauung* became a mush of dissatisfaction, reaction, abreaction. The fiction grew soft and sloppy.

Mick has stopped screaming but Delphine doesn't notice. She is almost there, now.

Delphine jerks the door open.

Oh horror!

Mick, as she suspected from the moment of his first scream, is being murdered. Or perhaps he is now already dead. He's slumped forwards, his head hanging down limply over his clavicle. His breast is a bubbling stew of blood. Delphine was half-right about the killer. Her prime suspect is Dippy, and sure enough it's his second wife who stands before him, twisting a bloodied knife into his chest. Dippy's rhythm has all the regularity of a machine. She is stirring a cauldron, like a witch at Halloween. Her face is fierce, clenched, exultant.

What Wife Number Three didn't expect is to find that Dippy has an accomplice. It takes Delphine a moment or so to recognise the other blood-splashed person. The identification shakes her to the core. That big, heavy woman who stands behind Mick, holding him in her massive vice-like grip and pinioning his arms behind him, is Gwynned. *Gwynned Hooley, his first wife!*

Delphine has only ever seen her in photographs. Gwynned's face is still just recognisable, though it has thickened and cracked with age. The worn face and the straggly unkempt hair are less of a shock than the woman's girth. She's enormous! She must have tripled in size since the days of being the first Mrs Owen. She strongly reminded Delphine of the Sumo-wrestler-sized oriental assassin who John Wick has great difficulty in subduing towards the end of *John Wick: Chapter Two*.

As Delphine stands there, paralysed with shock, staring, Wife Number One lets go of Mick's body. The corpse slumps to the floor, leaking blood. It reminds Delphine of that marvellous occasion they went to see a Jacobean revenge tragedy at the Menier Chocolate Factory on Southwark Street. Mick was grumpy because she hadn't obtained front row seats but a pair three rows back. As it happened this was a mercy. A couple in the front row were inadvertently splattered. The stage blood had been copious and very squirty. Delphine frowns. What was it, the play? Those revenge tragedies all blur together. *The White Devil*? She really can't remember. They still have the programme, she's sure of that. Mick chucks nowt out.

Dippy lets the blood-soaked knife drop. She chuckles fiendishly and begins to peel off her wet clothes. Gwynned does the same. Soon they are both naked. Their skin seems strangely colourless against the scarlet backdrop. Wife Number One seems enormous next to Wife Number Two. Gwynned's swinging breasts are like sacks of potatoes.[26] Her torso is the

[26] 'Gwynned's swinging breasts are like sacks of potatoes': A very dubious simile. A sack of potatoes is lumpy and uneven. Besides, the

size of a pillar box. A sharp contrast to Dippy, who is still tall and thin, though her small breasts are now a little wrinkled, like peaches past their sell-by date. Her hair is still magnificent but there has been a recent fall of snow.

Dippy blows Delphine a kiss. Gwynedd touches herself suggestively. The two women began to writhe on the wet carpet. Soon they are copiously smeared in the dead man's blood. It would be the perfect moment to recite something from *Macbeth.*

'Join us,' whispers Dippy, opening those tall legs of hers and beckoning with a curled forefinger. Her shaved gash seems very large. It glistens, like a split fruit.

Delphine, freshly aware of her own nudity, feels a strange thrill begin to spread from the region of her groin. Her pulse accelerates wildly. 'Mon Dieu,' she breathes. As if in a dream she moves forward and sinks to the floor.

Soon it is as if a pale twelve-limbed deep-sea creature is undergoing some strange convulsion involving gasps, shudderings, cries, the loose ecstatic inadvertent breaking of wind...

How alike are the groans of love to the groans of the dying...

But no, life is not, for most of us, a mash-up of scenes from a movie by Sam Peckinpah and Catherine Breillat.[27] This, above, is not what happened. What happened was entirely different.

Delphine jerks the door open. She sees Mick standing there, close to his desk. With the exception of his laptop, it has been swept clean. The carpet is strewn with ballpoint pens, pencils,

intelligent and alert reader will surely ask: what variety? Maris Piper? King Edward? Charlotte? Sweet? Baking? New?

[27] Sam Peckinpah (1925-1984), American film director; Catherine Breillat (b. 1948), French filmmaker. Although its politics are dubious there is no doubting the immense dramatic power of the bloody end to Peckinpah's masterpiece, *The Wild Bunch.* The end of *Cross of Iron* is also memorable. *Bring Me the Head of Alfredo Garcia* is another classic, which no footnote aspiring to authority can afford to omit. As for Catherine Breillat: the allusion, plainly, is to *Anatomie de l'enfer.*

a lined pad of A4, some sheets of typing paper, and half a dozen paperbacks. He is trembling, very pale, evidently unable to speak.[28]

But there is no one with him!

Whatever has happened in this small room has happened to him alone. And then, suddenly, Delphine understands. Mick points at the Covarrubias upholstered chaise longue. His mobile phone is lying there, close to the headboard. He has received a message of such enormity that in an anguished response he has hurled it there and swept everything from his desk.

[28] 'unable to speak': This was a unique condition for an author who spoke his mind on numerous occasions, in interviews and newspaper columns and from the stage at innumerable conferences and cultural events. Mick Owen's fluency and loquacity were never in doubt. This, of course, needs to be distinguished from his *voluntary* silences. Although *Mick's Take* was acclaimed by the lackeys of the capitalist media, what was striking about its account of the years since 1945 was what it chose to blank out. The great Grunwick strike of 1976-78. Violent repression in the torture state of Bahrain, fully backed and equipped by the UK and USA. Similar support for the regime in Oman. Mick Owen could be relied upon to bleat about Ukraine but had zilch to say about British and American efforts to thwart socialism and democracy in Venezuela. His contribution to the great anti-Iraq war demonstration of 15 February 2003 was to shun it and then write a poisonously reactionary novel, *Sunday Blues*, which attacked the Left. The deportation of the Chagos islanders – one of the great British crimes of the post-war era – remained outside Mick Owen's field of vision. The Palestinians, of course, could never expect anything more from the novelist than banal platitudes of the sort which would attract not a squeak of objection from that screeching, bullying mob of Zionists which policed public utterance on this subject. Mick Owen's entire career was punctuated by off-screen atrocity, from small events to gigantic ones, yet his conscience was stirred only by ones acceptable to the corporate media. Although he was living just a few miles away he did not know about events in Southall on 23 April 1979 – or if he did, chose to say nothing. The phrase 'the Jakarta method' meant nothing at all to him. He was every inch a chest-thumping dewy-eyed *Guardian* liberal.

His screams, she now comprehends, were not screams of agony in response to physical pain, or an attacker plunging a knife into that vast network of veins and nerves which lies below smooth skin, but altogether different in origin. He has received some very bad news. It is information which hurts.

And he is still in shock. All he can do is point, mutely.

Delphine moves across the room to the phone to find out what has happened to reduce her usually eloquent husband to this condition.

Just above the chaise longue is the framed photograph of Mick, kneeling. His head is bowed and his bent knee is propped up by a stool capped with a red cushion. Her Royal Highness the Princess Anne gently brushes his shoulder with the sword. Arise, Sir Michael Owen!

A shame both his parents were dead. They would have been so proud. It was the greatest moment of his life (and one in the eye for all those ghastly bloggers!). Delphine in the audience looked absolutely stunning. She was the most beautiful woman in the room.

They had exchanged a few words, the Princess and the novelist. Up close he was suddenly aware of how prominent her upper teeth were. No wonder she loved horses. The Princess's breath was hot and thick and smelled of Spearmint. She had said – he could remember every word of this acutely memorable, undeniably historic and marvellously spectacular, occasion – 'They tell me you're an important novelist and good for exports. I'm afraid I don't have any time for books. Far too busy!' She cast the radiance of her smile upon him. He felt it spread over him like honey. It was sweet, it was golden.

He felt re-energised. In his younger days he had subscribed to the standard prejudices of his peer group. The royals were parasites and spongers. They were the quintessence of a degenerate ruling elite. The best solution was the Bolshevik one. *Bang, bang, bang!* Not just the family but also those sycophantic liveried servants. And especially those stupid little yapping dogs. *Bang, bang, bang*! But now he had matured –

unlike some of his old associates, who had dropped away into their drab little lives, snapping on social media that his lurch into reaction was an expression of seduction by the system: his wealth, his properties, his privileged lifestyle, his association with High Court judges, Chief Constables, newspaper proprietors and the like.

Not all that long ago, strolling past the marketplace in Norwich, Mick had suddenly realised that the scruffy, stooped figure clutching an unsold bundle of *Socialist Worker* and shouting 'Smash the Tories!' was Geoff. Geoff who decades ago had turned up for Alan Burns's creative writing seminar and recited a poem about Lenin. (Hugh MacDiarmid he wasn't.)[29] Yes, Geoff, who had once given him a lift in his little red mini all the way to Brighton. Geoff with a ponytail. In those days Geoff had been with the Spartacus League. In subsequent years he had evidently made a minor adjustment to his Far Left politics. Geoff still had the ponytail, but now it was grey and his hair was coarse and wiry. As he approached Geoff stared at him hopefully, sensing a sale. But Mick walked on by. It had only been an experiment to see if Geoff recognised him. But his old associate simply gazed at him blankly.

It was the same with other pensioners of that city. That small thin woman with white hair lapping her shoulders, who was towing a poodle in a tartan waistcoat – could that possibly be Sheila, the geography first year whom he had led upstairs at a party on Havelock Road? He remembered how in the morning she had cried. And that grotesque creature, monstrously obese and dragging herself along with a crutch – was that Dolly? She had been large, even back in 1973, but voluptuously so. He had once had sex with her in a lavatory cubicle of the Arts Block. They had snapped the toilet seat. By the time their exertions were over the connection to the cistern was damaged. They stumbled away from the scene of the crime red-faced and

[29] 'Hugh MacDiarmid he wasn't': Probably an allusion to the great Scottish poet's 'Second Hymn to Lenin', which begins with a timeless truth: *Ah, Lenin, you were richt.*

giggling, as a slow surge of water spread out from beneath the door and began to move down the corridor like a slowly unrolling carpet.

Dolly also failed to recognise him, flopping past him like a wounded animal, dragging along her massively inflated torso, wheezy and lame and weak. Odd how some names always came back to haunt you. As he shivered in that large palatial room waiting for his knighthood to be bestowed, the Band of the Coldstream Guards played Her Royal Highness's favourite music – an orchestral medley from *Hello, Dolly!*

Mick no longer drank to excess. It was the consequence of that other royal occasion in his life.

The invitation to Highgrove had clashed with a trip to Helsinki – his first six books were being republished in paperback, in a new translation. He was scheduled to do a reading and give interviews. He cancelled it. Dinner at Highgrove with Charles Windsor would be far more interesting, he decided. By now his sales and critical reputation were such that he could afford to annoy his publishers once in a while.

It turned out to be one of the worst nights of his life – or at least, one of the ones he most regretted. He drove there alone (the silver copperplate message on the monogrammed card pointedly did not invite him to bring a companion). At the gate he had to show his invitation and his passport to a policeman, then he was waved on to the next barrier. There he had to park over a sort of cattle grid. Instructed to get out of the car, he was obliged to step through an airport-style metal security frame. Having passed through without triggering the alarm, he waited while the Merc was scanned from below. A bar of light traversed the exhaust, the catalytic converter and all the mysterious dirt-encrusted panels of the underside. It was like watching a giant photocopier in action.

After that he was free to drive on towards the house.

It was clear that the police officers on duty were not readers of literary fiction or *The Guardian*. They simply had no idea of who he was. Had they been aware they would surely have requested selfies or an autograph. He was always gracious when such demands were made, no matter how irritating. His smile, now 55 per cent implants, was all over social media. He was generally adored, apart from the usual fringe of trolls, Trotskyists, creationists and envious critics seeking to puncture his reputation.

Beside the long drive at Highgrove, under arc lights, could be seen a dozen Gurkhas in shorts. They were on their knees, holding tiny silver scissors. They were trimming the lawn blade by blade. It was like a scene from one of those awful European 'experimental' films.

Mick was greatly looking forward to meeting Charles. The prospect did not intimidate him. He had in recent years dined with the Archbishops of Canterbury and York, the Chief Rabbi, a recently retired Commissioner of the Metropolitan Police, a High Court judge, the Lord Chief Justice, and two retired generals, as well as many lesser figures. On every occasion he felt that they were flattered to meet him. He added lustre to their proceedings. He could be relied upon for civilised conversation. There was a sense that, no matter what their differences – nuances of politics, the matter of religious belief or its absence – they had in common a number of essential values.

Alas, the evening with the future King was not a success. At the side of the house a flunkey in livery took his keys to park the Mercedes. Another liveried flunky led him into a side room and gravely informed him that he must only ever address his host as "Your Royal Highness" or – one or two times but no more – as "sir". *Never* – the flunky raised his forefinger in warning – as Charles or Prince. (Prince was what some people called their dog.)

Usually when Mick met prominent members of the Establishment they had always read at least one of his books. Usually it was *Restitution*. Sometimes he suspected they had only seen the movie. That evening with Charles it was different. He began to wonder if the Prince knew much about him, other than that he was some sort of celebrity with an expressed interest in the environment. Had Charles actually read *any* of his books? As the evening wore on he rather doubted it. It didn't sound as if he'd seen any of the adaptations either. In fact he hadn't even got a flunkey to find out more and supply him with a plot précis of one or two of the more famous titles. Charles, it became clear, was a monstrous narcissist. He was lazy and superficial. He genuinely believed he was a man of infinite wisdom and understanding. In reality he was like a small child, requiring only attention, diversion and complete agreement in all matters. Everything had to be *Yes*. *No* and even the smallest dissent was entirely out of the question. *No* led to tantrums and brimming eyes and red-faced fury. Everything had to go his way.

That evening Mick was not the only guest. The others were well-known environmentalists: Jon Porridge of The Greening Institute, *The Guardian* columnist Jorge Bleriot, Tim Bland, Director of The Prince's Environmental Fund (bankrolled by suitcases filled with Saudi cash, it was claimed). Mick had not been invited because of his impressive literary accomplishments, or because of his personal contribution to peace in the Middle East. No. It was simply and solely because of his recent high-profile environmentalism. He'd attended various conferences around the world. He had spent two weeks in Antarctica, becoming acquainted with calving ice and polar bears. In Tokyo he had called for curbs on aviation. In New Zealand he deplored the cult of personal consumption and said we must all learn to live simpler lives. In Jerusalem he had informed his hosts that the Palestinians needed to renounce violence and recognise that the threat to their existence was not a Jewish state but rising sea levels. The Gaza Strip would become the sea bed unless we all pulled together and learned to respect difference. In Brazil he begged the audience to protect the rain forest. In Los Angeles he praised the great strides being made in electric car manufacture.

In one year alone he flew to more environmental conferences than literary festivals.

That night it was the wine that made him reckless. The flunkey behind him kept springing forward to keep his glass topped up. The flunkey liked being in motion. Being in motion was preferable to standing silently against the wall, motionless as a guardsman outside Buckingham Palace. And the wine the Prince served really was awfully good. It was like liquid velvet.

Somehow the conversation had jumped from fossil fuels to architecture. It was in retrospect very unfortunate that Mick had only recently returned from the Bridport Arts Festival. He'd driven back to London, obeying his satnav. For some reason the device had the voice of a female New Yorker. His spectral guide advised him to avoid the Dorchester by-pass and instead take the short cut through town. Sound advice – but a route that involves starting at the roundabouts of Poundbury and two or three minutes of proximity to Charles's sub-Georgian toy town fantasy. If you follow the sign to Queen Mother Square then you've missed your turn and will need to go back, for this route is a dead end.

Jon Porridge, for whom the adjective 'sycophantic' might have been freshly coined, was blathering about how inspirational His Royal Highness's leadership on environmental issues had been when Mick cut rudely cut in. 'I was in Poundland only recently...'

The table fell silent. At first the other three guests thought he was referring to that discount store favoured by poor people. They had heard of it, although none of them had ever been inside one. Bleriot remembered he had once walked past a branch in a shopping centre in a shabby part London.

Only one person present understood the small slippage in the intended pronunciation. Mick saw the Prince wince at the word, as if someone had pricked him with a needle. Then he began to glower. His face at first just florid turned a deeper shade of beetroot.

'Carriage lamps,' Mick continued. 'I don't see the point of putting carriage lamps outside a modern building. After all, nobody rides around in a horse-drawn carriage anymore, do they?'

There was a long silence.

'Except your lot of course,' he added, nodding at the empurpled Prince, and then adding to his addition: 'Royal occasions and all that. The Mall. By the way, whatever happened to that ridiculous golden coach?'

Mick drained his glass and in the blink of an eyelid a hand to his right was tilting a bottle. He watched the miniature waterfall as it hit the base of his glass and briefly frothed. He took some more sips, aware that the room now contained silence at full volume, with an atmosphere that reminded him of his trip to Antarctica. The silence; the extreme cold.

Jorge Bleriot attempted a diversion. 'About rewilding, your Royal Highness.'

But Charles was in no mood to be diverted. He trembled. He was furious. He spat the words out.

'*Poundbury* is about *style.* About *heritage.* About a kind of knowledge that is written in blood. In *royal* blood.' He added with a sniff: 'I designed it myself. Down to the last heritage feature. *Including the lamps.*'

Strangely Mick's glass was empty. But once again there was a hand bobbing down beside his brow, then pausing by his cheek, and, cradling another bottle, gently moving forwards to refresh the empty receptacle. Mick glanced up and saw what he felt was a twinkle in the man's eyes and the hint of a smile at the corners of his mouth. He felt this fellow, despite his absurd pantomime costume, was truly on his side. This was good. This was how revolutions began. He started to feel like he was that person who'd first summoned the courage to boo the dictator Nicolae Ceauşescu in Palace Square on 21 December 1989. Charles's mother, Mick remembered, had been the recipient of the Order of the Star of the Socialist Republic of Romania, just as she had awarded the dictator the Knight Grand Cross of the Most Honourable Order of the Bath.

Mick raised his glass, took a series of swigs, and returned to battle. 'Carriage lamps on the ground floor – bad enough in the twenty-first century. But in your Poundland – sorry, Poundburg – sorry, borough – sorry, *bury* – in your toy suburb there are carriage lamps on the first floor as well. Who are they for? Father Christmas? The phantom horseman? Christ, I've never seen anything so mind-numbingly stupid in all my life.'

He knew at once he had gone too far. He cleared his throat.

Best to apologise at once. The others around the table looked aghast, as if a rattlesnake had suddenly hopped on to the table and raised its swaying reptilian head, considering whom to bite first.

The Prince said thickly: 'This really is appalling. Beastly. Stinking, in fact.' He stood up and added, 'Stinking. Absolutely bloody stinking.' He turned and something on his apparel – a hook, a button, a low-slung medal – caught on the tablecloth. As the Prince of Wales moved away he inadvertently jerked the cloth. Like flimsy finely balanced structures in an earthquake, every wine glass toppled.

Red wine spilt like fresh blood.

White wine surged like – like – like spilled white wine.

A plate flipped off and crashed across the floor. More followed. It reminded Mick of a scene in *Titanic*. Cutlery clattered after the plates, like dogs pursuing their owners.

There was no doubt about it. This ship was doomed. The Prince stamped from the room, swearing. He towed the tablecloth after him like a bloodied tail. You wanted to release him into the surrounding fields and send the local hunt in pursuit.

The Prince of Wales slammed the door after him.

'You absolute bloody idiot!' screamed Bleriot in the silence that followed the Prince's departure from the room.

'Do you realise what you've done?' howled Porridge. 'Do you honestly think any of us are going to get an honour after this?'

'It's alright for you,' snarled Bland. He was shaking. 'You've got your bloody knighthood. But some of us haven't even got our MBE yet. You fool. You complete and total fool.'

'You've set the cause of environmentalism back by a decade!' shrieked Bleriot. 'When a tornado destroys your house you might like to reflect on your own role in making that happen.'

Mick stood. 'Oh, just fuck off, the bloody lot of you.' He swayed as he said it. He had to readjust the position of his feet. The room had a slight tilt, a slow spin. At moments like this it was easy to believe that the world was round and you were balanced on a globe rotating in a black void. Science had always been dear to his intelligent and rational heart.

The door opened again. But it was not Charles. It was the flunkey who'd given them their behaviour instructions on the way in. His face was grim. 'His Royal Highness wishes you all to depart,' he said brusquely.

Bleriot said: 'It wasn't *us*.' He pointed an accusing finger. 'It was *him*.'

A chorus of agreement.

Mick didn't care. The footman who had served him his wine loomed before him. To his astonishment the fellow gave him a quick, furtive wink.

Mick felt his inner glow glow more warmly. Of course! The chap admired him for standing up to the Prince.

Then, mysteriously, he was outside, under the stars, and his car was sliding to a halt in front of him. Pure magic. He climbed inside.

He had driven eight miles when the blue flashing light appeared behind him.

When the police officer appeared beside his window Mick was calm. He said: 'A jumbo burger with cheese and an extra portion of chips, please.'

It was not his fault that he was not at the drive-in McDonald's off the A12 was it? He was breathalysed, handcuffed, imprisoned. He felt like Nelson Mandela.

Delphine, mercifully, was in Paris.

In the morning Sandra was there to collect him. He broached the idea of a prison diary but she said she felt it was best if they hushed the whole thing up. It might dent his image.

Later, when he was sober and his head no longer throbbed, he agreed. She was his rock, as well as his roll. He pleaded guilty. Six points and a fine equivalent to five second's royalties. Manageable.

Astonishingly, the newspapers never found out. There was no reporter in court – cuts had taken their toll on local journalism – and Michael Owen is a very common name. It was plain that neither the police nor the magistrates had any idea who he was. It was just like the time a police car in the States was sent to apprehend a suspicious hooded figure seen walking through an affluent white neighbourhood. The pedestrian gruffly told them his name was Bob Dylan, which meant nothing whatever to the cops. They put him in the car and took him back to check out his story at the expensive hotel where this scruffy prospective thief implausibly claimed to be staying.

It was Mick's second major failure with a celebrity.

Invited to number 10, he was hoping to meet Gwyneth Paltrow, but instead he was seated next to the Belgian ambassador, who looked exactly as you would expect the Belgian ambassador to look. A description would be superfluous. Words would be a barren expenditure. Grey would be a wholly unnecessary adjectival extravagance.

Incredibly, the fellow had plainly never heard of Mick Owen and his novels. The novelist was trapped beside a pudgy diplomatic bore. Astonishingly, the diplomat knew little of Magritte and had never heard of Edith Cavell. The only topic they could truly meet on was the Tintin books. They were both great fans of *The Secret of the Unicorn.*

Later he actually saw Gwyneth Paltrow, but she was being monopolised by Salman, while a circle of admirers stood around then, collecting the pearls of their conversation.

He stood there, momentarily alone, back to the wall, when the Prime Minister swooped.

Tony Blair, with his strange grimace and oddly restless flickering eyes. The grimace belonged to a squirrel suffering from acute constipation. The eyes were those of a predatory snake.

Blair slithered up to him and manufactured a kind of stretched smile.

'You must be packing some heat under your jacket, eh?' the Prime Minister chuckled. His eyes did a jig and he bobbed his head like a pigeon, expectant, waiting for a reply. Now he was more weasel than squirrel. At close range his breath had the odour of the public drains in St Anton am Arlberg.

It took some time to establish that, no, Mick was not Salman Rushdie's bodyguard. Once this misunderstanding was cleared away and Mick had explained who he was, Blair claimed to be an enormous fan of his books. But when pointedly asked which was his favourite Mick Owen novel the Prime Minister, his smile now that of the elongated mouth of the first victim at the moment of fatal impact in a slasher movie, said it had been really great meeting him – really, really great – but Mick would understand that he mustn't neglect his other guests. Blair briefly pumped his guest's hand with great energy. Then he darted away like a very common specimen of London vermin.

A moment later Mick observed that the Prime Minister was engaged with a moronic Irish rock star, the lead singer of a group whose music was a banal, calculated synthesis of basic sixties rock with a half-baked surrealism that miserably failed to equal the two Procol Harum classics. The sales of this melodic throbbing cloudy derivative drivel were of a magnitude a novelist could only dream of – unless your name was Marie Corelli, Agatha Christie, Jean Plaidy, or J. K. Rowling.

As Delphine moves across the room to Mick's phone to find out exactly what has happened – what is the terrible message on that tiny screen? – she is struck by how much her husband resembles the figure in Edvard Munch's 'The Scream'. His hands are clapped over his ears. His eyes are strangely circular, distorted by horror. His stretched mouth is the shape of an egg. His slender face is pale and skull-like. Now, instead of screaming, he simply whimpers.

What is this awful thing which has occurred? Another 9/11? Some great slaughter in which affluent American professionals have died? Or white Europeans? Or Israelis?

She reaches the phone.

She snatches it up and presses the thin wedge of plastic that refreshes the dark screen.

And there it is.

The year is 2017 and a shattering event has just taken place.

It is like a vat of boiling oil tipped down from a besieged castle as Mick bravely ascends a tall wooden ladder to the battlements.

It's like a chip pan of seething fat emptied by an enraged lover over her cheating partner.

It's like a bullet to the heart.

It's like that moment towards the end of *Westworld* (1973) when the hunted man with a moustache throws acid into Yul Brynner's face.

The screen comes back to life in glowing colour.

And there it is, unambiguous, stark, inescapable.

BREAKING NEWS.
KAZUO ISHIGURO AWARDED
NOBEL PRIZE FOR LITERATURE.

Delphine flinches. She feels her husband's acute and terrible pain.

'Oh my poor darling!'

She returns across the vast space of that ice-cold room to take him in her arms. This is far, far worse than that awful, dreadful, humiliating occasion when *Woman with a Cat* failed to win The Barker Prize. 'My poor, poor baby.'

But he pushes her away. He's pale; trembling. And now his voice returns. A rich voice, filled with passionate intensity. 'Fucking Ishiguro! That fucking mediocrity! He's only published seven novels for Christ's sake! *Seven!* Those fucking Swedes! Shits! Cunts![30] Arseholes! They wouldn't know a fucking work of literature if it kicked them in the fucking balls!'

'Darling...' She tries to squeeze his hand; to kiss him. But still he rebuffs her. His speech continues to release a series of

[30] 'Cunts!' It is curiously revelatory of American hegemony in the sphere of software and its repressed, authoritarian instincts, that in the year 2023 spellcheck should refuse to recognise 'cunts' as a word, serving up instead the following absurd alternatives: cants, cents, counts, cuts, cults. Of the five, 'cents' is perhaps the one to pay most attention to.

nouns, but increasingly they arrive chained to adjectives. Now the members of the Swedish Academy are not simply cunts but total cunts, not shits but complete shits.

His face is like the screen on his phone. The colour has returned. His cheeks burn. His nose appears luminous, like that of The Dong. His brow seems oddly yellowish.

'I'm going for a walk,' he hisses. '*Alone*.'

She knows better than to challenge his choice. She steps back to allow him pass her. A moment later she hears him clattering down the circular staircase.

It is stiflingly hot in his study. She collects the papers strewn across the carpet, then opens two of the windows. A cooling breeze enters and caresses her. Somewhere below a blackbird sings.

Suddenly Delphine feels very sexy and in need of relaxation. Heat and wind often have that effect upon her.

She stretches back on the chaise longue and opens her legs. Her right hand settles on her crotch like a hungry crab crouched on a seaweed-coated rock. She probes for meat and quickly finds it. Slow repetitive movement; an acceleration; a sweet shivering; shuddering; a sequence of small expulsions of oxygen; several barely audible grunts.

A delicate flush on her cheeks as she stands and goes to the nearest open window. She looks down.

Mick is now crossing the lawn, going past the pool and heading for the woods.

He is carrying his recently acquired shotgun. She suddenly recalls that in recent weeks he has been reading a lot of Hemingway.

Part Two:
Fire

1

Five years later.

He lay in the dark, uncertain of the time. He reached out and flicked the transistor radio on. He was just in time for the headlines.

The opening words hit him like the blunt end of a hammer. 'Britain's greatest writer is dead. Literary agent Ben Pike issued a statement today announcing the death of –'

Mick jerked forward in shock. The spasm caused him inadvertently to flick the machine off. His heart burned and bounced around hotly, painfully, inside him. A maniac in the next room was battering a drum.

He was dead. This was a most unpleasant surprise. He lay in the darkness, trying to make sense of it. How had this happened? Had he died in his sleep, quite unexpectedly, as old folk sometimes did? Bertrand Russell had departed by that route. Or had he suffered a massive stroke and been instantly plummeted into the afterlife? Cardiac arrest (a distressing term, which always made him think of rough, coarse, violent members of the notorious Metropolitan Police force)?

The ghost of his stomach still held bubbling acid in its pit. His deceased bowels still seemed to churn. Though dead, his mind scampered to and fro, batting thoughts like party balloons.

Ben Pike had been Mick's new literary agent ever since Sandra Locke had died a decade earlier. Poor Sandra. She had parked on a double yellow line while she popped into Selfridges and when she came back a traffic warden was attaching a penalty notice to her windscreen. Even now the circumstances were vague. Words had been exchanged. The warden, a person of colour, claimed that Sandra had racially abused him. In response, the warden denied saying anything other than what he had been trained to say. A straightforward explanation as to the nature of the parking offence, with an added reference to the appeals service for those who felt an injustice had been committed. Witnesses described an angry old white woman with flushed cheeks. She had snatched the parking ticket and hurled it at its issuer. The man had remained calm and dignified. He had spoken in an apparently reasonable and moderate manner. Next thing Sandra had been observed clawing at her chest, as if attempting to excavate something. Then she dropped to the ground like Bill at the end of Tarantino's masterpiece. Dead. A massive heart attack. All very sad. Hundreds turned out for the memorial service at St Bride's. Mick had spoken, of course. He had compared their trajectories, Sandra's and his own, from the margins to the centre. He had praised her extravagantly. Without her – without her remarkable understanding of how literature might be shaped for the average guy at an airport bookstall – he, Mick Owen, would never have become the writer he was today.

Afterwards he'd dumped The Sandra Locke Agency and switched to The Big Fish Agency and Ben Pike. Ben, who handled other giants, was infamous for his ruthlessness and bullying. Mick admired him tremendously for his business acumen. They rarely discussed anything more than plot and theme. Ben had his eye on the zeitgeist. Within two years he'd doubled Mick's income stream. Ben was unenthusiastic about Sam Quiggly's biography but decided to ignore it. Once Mick was dead he'd put lawyers on to the contract. He was confident he could edge Quiggly out and find a better biographer. A woman would be good. But all that lay in the future... And now that moment had arrived. Mick was pleased to hear Ben speak of him so highly. But then he knew in his now unpumping heart that that was just PR. Ben smelled extra sales.

When Mick's nerves had settled he reflected that he'd just been listening to the radio. How was that possible?

And then he remembered. This was all exactly as Dennis Wheatley had described it in *The Ka of Gifford Hilary*. He'd first read it at the age of thirteen. It had affected him like almost nothing else he had ever read (apart from Space-Ranger Colin's defeat of the Martians in *Mariners of Space*).

Dreaming, Mick learned, was just a rehearsal for death. It took you into another dimension – a world of spirits.

Wheatley showed how the body died but the soul – your Ka – lived on. You slowly floated upward from your spent flesh to ceiling level. There you waited quietly and invisibly in a corner, alongside the spider that lived there. You could watch as Delphine entered and discovered your body. You would be able to see her cry of anxiety – of horror. But then you remembered she was in Paris. Someone else would have to discover your corpse. Perhaps a bad smell would alert them.

The details did not matter. You were dead. You no longer had any responsibilities to discharge. You could afford to be patient. You were in no hurry. You had eternity ahead of you.

It was actually very interesting, seeing what happened. Mick regretted being unable to write about it. The ultimate autofictional text! He would call it *The Undiscovered Country* – a brilliant and clever title! His brightest readers would feel a little tingle, knowing where it came from.

But then he remembered that that bastard Julian Mitchell had got there first. An experimental novel of the sixties. It hadn't sold and it was now long forgotten. He could vaguely recall the cover of the paperback. A naked woman fashioned out of heavily eroded limestone lay on her side like a petrified figure at Pompeii. It wasn't a book he'd bought. Experimental writing – the words made him shudder.[31]

He knew if he used the title some miserable little prick would spot it and all the old charges of plagiarism would boil to the surface once more, like an ascending gas-filled corpse carving open the surface of a black lake in a crime story. But then he remembered he was dead – so no worries.

He looked forward to a drama worthy of any realist novel. The discovery of his body! – the doctor! – the two men from

[31] 'A naked woman fashioned out of heavily eroded limestone': see Julian Mitchell, *The Undiscovered Country* (London: Constable, 1968). The cover which Mick remembers is that of the 1970 Panther edition, which pitched it as 'One of the most unusual novels to appear in years – entertaining, amusing, outrageous.'

the undertakers! These last two characters encased your cold stiff flesh in a large black plastic bag. This they covered in a purple blanket with gold frills along the edge. You were taken out on a stretcher, feet first, and slid into the back of a van about the size of the ones used by Amazon Prime. But the flanks of the van were black, with no wording.

Later, when your earthly body had departed for its brief residency at the funeral parlour, what was left of you could go for a stroll – or at least, a drift. You could pass through walls, just like the advanced model terminator in the second instalment of that marvellous franchise. And as Dennis Wheatley had noted, you could accompany a woman to the lavatory and scrutinise her activities, while she was wholly oblivious of your surveillance.

The available voyeurism was unlimited. You could drop by to see old friends and investigate their sex lives from the bedside. The downside was that you would never again experience an erection or an orgasm. You no longer required food and drink, as you were now spectral. You couldn't smell anything, or feel rain. On the plus side, no more constipation, diarrhoea or uncontrollable farting. And no more toothache!

He lay there, cogitating. It was a habit which went back to early adolescence.

Tomorrow he would go out and read his obituaries and the tributes from friends. He knew his death would be good for sales. Sales always rocketed in the immediate aftermath of a famous author's death. Readers got a strange thrill from the knowledge that they were alive, whereas the author was freshly deceased. He would never add a single new word to any page.

Mick's hand slid down the sheet. Oddly he still seemed to possess a set of genitals. Perhaps he was still resting in his abandoned flesh. His etheric body had yet to achieve lift-off. It was slumbering inside the sleeping bag of his still warm corpse.

Or perhaps Wheatley was wrong...

Mick suddenly remembered Dippy's copy of *The Tibetan Book of the Dead*, which was nowhere near as well known as the Egyptian one. In the early days of their relationship, when he was anxious to please her in everything, he had read her copy. He vaguely remembered it as a clogged and cluttered text which piled immense esoteric detail around some simple ideas. After death, apparently, you went through three stages of afterlife, called The Bardo, a term which decades later had received some wider publicity after an American writer whose name he couldn't remember had won the Booker Prize for *Lincoln in the Bardo*. Mick hadn't read it. He had zero interest in pre-twentieth century American presidents. He barely remembered Dippy's heavily annotated edition of *The Tibetan Book of the Dead*.[32]

He did recall that the First Bardo lasted for three-and-a-half days (a curiously precise period of time). In this state you don't know you are dead. In the Second Bardo you realise you are dead but still think you have a biological body in the afterlife. When you find out you don't, you feel a great yearning to possess one. Somehow you find your way into the Third Bardo, where you seek Rebirth. Unless you've plunged straight into Nirvana, you are reborn in human form.

It was all terribly complicated, and it involved visions of lakes, cattle, mansions, temples and rocky landscapes, along with advice about what to visit and what to avoid at all costs. Dippy pronounced the book blissful and enlightening. She seemed confident of a smooth journey along these three great connected spiritual motorways leading to a Birmingham of the soul. *The Tibetan Book of the Dead* combined the route knowledge of satnav with the up to date travel tips of Google.

Mick, a materialist and a sceptic, wondered how anyone had managed to do the journey in reverse and supply this route map. Anyway, Dippy's cherished volume couldn't be right because he knew he was dead already. He didn't have to wait another four days to find out. Or perhaps his was an

[32] Dippy's copy of *The Tibetan Book of the Dead* was the 1951 second impression of the text edited by W. Y. Evans-Wentz and published by OUP, with a Preface the final paragraph of which begins, "Whilst this Preface is being written it is Easter in California." The year of the Easter in question was 1948 – the year of Mick Owen's birth.

exceptionally enlightened and deeply spiritual soul. If true, this meant he was well ahead of the rest of the simultaneously deceased. If so, Nirvana beckoned.

He hoped so.

He'd enjoy chatting to Kurt Cobain.

2

Strangely, Mick found he could lift his arm. He was fairly sure *The Tibetan Book of the Dead* hadn't mentioned that aspect of the afterlife. He reached out and turned the radio back on. The 'on' button responded to his touch. Surely that shouldn't happen?

The conversation was still all about him. His death was a massive story, just as he'd always known it would be. First Queen Elizabeth II and now him. It was a terrific time for celebrity departures.

A male voice with a commanding, authoritative tone marinated at a top public school and then Cambridge was gushing about the finest English novels of recent times. But then, mysteriously, the voice said, 'She was, quite simply, our greatest living British writer.'

She?

Mick was utterly bewildered. Was this a slip of the tongue? If not, who could be meant? Jo Rowling? Was she dead? Assassinated by a radical feminist with progressive views where self-identifying-gender lavatory access was concerned?

But now the voice was heaping praises on *Wolf Hall.* So! Not him at all and not Jo but Hilary Mantel! He was alive and she had expired. He was in his warm bed at his snug mews house in Knightsbridge and she was currently in a low temperature environment somewhere in Devon.

Phew!

Of course the Dame had always been vaguely unwell, but it was still a considerable shock. He'd met her a few times at book launches and literary festivals. She was a rather weird looking woman. Her strange doll's face with its massive frog eyes and a head perched on top of a body which resembled a chiffon-swathed pyramid. Mantel was both enormous and misshapen. A century ago she'd surely have been exhibited in the next cage to The Elephant Man.

The memory of their brief conversations vibrated in his head. That odd soft squeaky voice, like an enthusiastic yet hesitant schoolgirl with an impediment.

As for those books.

Mock-Tudor. Very popular in the suburbs.

Later he shaved, showered and coated his armpits and chest in pungent deodorant. He dressed, casual smart. It was 24 September 2022. The Queen was dead and only very recently buried. Val McDermid was being threatened with legal action by the Agatha Christie estate, which claimed copyright on the phrase 'the Queen of Crime'. And Dame Hilary was gone.

This was not a matter for grief. He barely knew Mantel. Mick sympathised, though. One felt, looking at the photographs, that sitting on a plastic toilet seat must have been a terrible ordeal for her. One knew from one's own experience that they could be thin and flimsy, with plastic bolts that came loose. There was always the risk of a sudden loosening of the foundations. An unexpected slippage, a sudden slither – next moment you might find yourself deposited on a cold hard floor dappled with other people's urine. You also would not want to smash whatever delicate and important network of bones supplied the foundations to the fat of one's buttocks.

He recalled Camilla Long's cruel but memorable description of Mantel as resembling a space hopper. (You could always rely on Camilla to make you laugh.)[33]

Poor old Hilary. Dead as a doornail (whatever that meant).

He would never allow this feeling to be articulated, not even in his diary, but he felt considerable elation. A private joy. There was the sweet knowledge that the competition had suddenly lessened.

It had been disappearing for quite some time now. Sebald, on the shimmering cusp of fame, gone for a cropper. A dismal way to die, meeting a lorry on a bend on that fume-drenched 'A' road between Beccles and Norwich.

[33] Camilla Elizabeth Long, b. 18 June 1978. A member of Rupert Murdoch's troupe of clowns. According to factsbuddy.com 'She is a woman of average stature.'

And many others. Old age gobbled them up (John Fowles). Sickness took a few (Malcom Bradbury dead at 68).

Iain Banks, gone before he was sixty.

Terry Pratchett, born the same year as Mick, gone.

John le Carré – about bloody time.

It was almost as if the Grim Reaper was a good mate, doing Mick a few favours now and then

But Margaret Atwood was still hanging on, even though nowadays she looked like a skull wearing an ill-fitting and badly moth-eaten wig. Lord, *how much longer?*

Mick thought how tragic it would be if Lee Child should find himself in a helicopter at three thousand feet when the Jesus bolt sheared in two.

Perhaps Ishiguro would gulp down an artichoke and the last five letters of that vegetable's name would turn into a tragically ironic description of his fate. (Fingers crossed.)

Collisions, lightning strikes, strokes, cardiac arrest, innumerable forms of cancer: these, he felt, were not for Mick Owen but for the others.

He smiled a Jack Nicholson smile.

In his fancy the great battlefield of contemporary literature was littered with the dead and dying. He wandered the field, examining each corpse and each gasping, fatally injured figure in turn. Some reached up, wanting him to take their hand. Philip Pullman? He flinched, brushed the wretch aside, and passed on.

His friends were naturally exempt.

Martin was still among the lusty living. Julian thrived. Craig ditto. And then of course there was Joanna. Mick was a superstar but she was an entire galaxy. No worries. Her readers were not the sort who would ever switch to the fiction of Mick Owen. Besides, she was now a good friend. Increasingly they saw eye-to-eye with each other on almost everything. Women and penises, for example.

But not everyone who endured was like they used to be. Alas for Salman, savagely knifed. He was alive, but an eye was gone; one hand floppy and useless.

Mick knew he could not share these dark thoughts with Delphine. She was soft and sentimental, as so many women are. She was protective of ants by the back door when he wanted to tip scalding water from a kettle. She would not allow him to spray a lingering wasp in the second guest bathroom. She said the insecticide not only left its tiny droplets afloat in the domestic air they breathed but also tormented the poor creature for an hour before its abdomen ceased to shudder and its whirring legs at last grew stiff. (Speed limits, mercifully, she had less respect for.)

Delphine was still grumpy about that day when the terrible news of Ishiguro's Nobel Prize broke. She had watched Mick as he headed for the woods with his shotgun, convinced he was going to do a Hemingway. In reality he just felt the need to kill a few animals. He managed to down a crow, blast a squirrel and slaughter seven rabbits. After that he felt much better. If *The Tibetan Book of the Dead* was true – he was quite certain it was bollocks, actually – there'd be a karmic bill to settle later. If so, he didn't care.

When he returned to the house that day she was sobbing and white-faced, convinced he was dead. It was delightful to know the prospect had that effect on her. She'd been so thrilled to see him come back to the house that she'd whispered he could do whatever he wanted. He whispered back. She blanched but permitted it.

Later, reflecting on Ishiguro's triumph, he'd managed a smile. 'Fuck it,' he said tenderly. 'Fuck those fucking Swedes. That crypto Jap creep's sales will never match mine.'

3

Now, five years later, he was still alive, Mantel was dead, and McDermid was being harassed by the Christie estate. Times sure were good! Plus his new novel, *Mick's Take*, had received the standard chorus of ecstatic reviews.

He went out that day with a spring in his step. He wore sunglasses and a baseball cap to disguise himself from his fans. This simple trick worked everywhere except Oxford.

He emerged from the sleepy mews, into a quiet Belgravian street, all tall creamy residences with twin pillar porches. Soon he was passing the spot where Field Marshall Sir Henry Wilson had been gunned down by a pair of Shinners a century ago. At the time it had been a national sensation. Today it was all but forgotten. Few people would know who Wilson was. At the assassination site there wasn't even a plaque. This had always surprised Mick. The guy had been an MP plus a greatly respected Great War general.

Mick gave a little shiver. Fame was a transient thing. One day you were a national figure. Then decades passed and you were forgotten.

At Buckingham Gate the street name plate was almost entirely obscured by flowers attached to the railings. A small crowd was reading the handwritten messages. It had been six days since the state funeral but the rotting remnants lingered on. Mick glanced at some of the cards and messages. Jenny Jing quoted the first two lines of Shakespeare's eighteenth sonnet and had drawn a crown and a lion. The lion reminded Mick of *The Wizard of Oz*. Someone, anonymous, thanked the Queen for her years of service, adding 'sleep tight'. Lucy E., plainly a child, had drawn a coloured-in Paddington Bear and written R.I.P.

Outside the Palace the crowd control barriers were not yet dismantled, funnelling tourists into the space before the railings. The Union Jack on the huge flagpole which rose from the roof of the Palace was at half mast. There was no one in residence, apart from servants. Tourists took photographs of the banal architecture and gazed with interest at the vast forecourt, empty apart from the distant toy guardsmen in their boxes and a group of three police officers, who cradled semi-automatic weapons as they chatted.

In interviews for *Mick's Take* he talked of his coronation mug, describing it as his oldest possession. A shrewd deflection of the topic. Others were less cleverly evasive and grovelled and slobbered like toadies at the court of any dictator. There should surely be a prize for Most Obsequious Novelist of the Year, and in 2022 there could be only one winner. Yes, the award goes to JW for her ludicrous and grotesque sob feature in (where else!) *The Guardian*, titled **She has been the one and only stable female in my life: Jeanette Winterson on mourning the Queen**.

Surely this heading was insulting to Suzie Orbach, who one understood was Winterson's partner? Or had they split? Mick had a suspicion that Winterson might not be the easiest of people to live with. He looked up her Wikipedia entry and discovered that, yes, the couple had separated.

Still a paid-up member of *The Guardian's* ever-shrinking readership, Mick read on. 'When I realised there was going to be an announcement about her death, I changed into black and waited. She deserved that. Part of us goes with her.'

Hark, ye! Give Jeanette any honour she'd like to choose – arse-licking on this scale surely merits it. But she'd already raked in an OBE and a CBE, so what baubles were left? Perhaps it would simply be best to get rid of the current incumbent and appoint her as the reigning Gentleman Usher of the Purple Rod. In the interests of diversity it was surely time for a woman to put her hand around that engorged object.

Reading Winterson's feature was to wade through a giant basin of strawberry-coated diarrhoea. 'Part of us goes with her. We mourn ourselves.' (Speak for yourself, Stupid.) 'My friend, the American writer A. M. Homes, also adopted, texted me immediately, and said: "We're orphans now."' FFS. The only word for this was *infantile*.

Not that Jeanette wept alone. That other intellectual titan,

David Beckham, made another pitch for that long overdue knighthood. He queued for many hours. (His skeletal wife wisely stayed at home, giving her bones a rest.) Tilda Swinton was photographed standing stiffly in front of the coffin, her head bowed. But then she'd always seemed rather weird. And among the other mourners was the lesser Hitchens, Peter. It's a long, long way from membership of the International Socialists to the end of the catafalque queue.

Mick made his way through the crowd and entered Green Park. Here a plain of decaying floral tributes looked like swathes of weed deposited after the passage of a tsunami. There were thousands of tributes. They had been gathered into heaps to await collection. Over to one side workers in fluorescent vests were already shovelling them into the back of a lorry.

Each heap had its little crowd of onlookers.

Innumerable bunches of daffodils and roses; Union Jacks of all sizes; hand-knitted soft toy animals, mainly bears; the flags of Canada, the USA, Italy. Poems. Letters. Candles. A THANK YOU from Chile. Printers had been busy pumping out upper case messages with large fonts. SHE LIVES IN OUR HEARTS. Repeated thanks for her life of service. Trees festooned with flags, messages, and helium balloons (semi-deflated; wrinkled). An arrangement of red and white chrysanthemums with a star and crescent. A card reading *Deepest Sympathy*. A paperback copy of *Paddington Takes the Air*. A child's letter beginning *Dear Your Late Majesty, I'm a Brownie*. A message from Sandra: 'You lit up our lives like a rainbow lights up the sky.' A Union Jack postcard bearing the words HONG KONG. Another print-out, using a fancy copperplate font: *You have gone from our sight but never from our hearts*. A cellophane-wrapped collage of photographs of the Queen, evidently clipped from a glossy magazine. A photograph of the flag of Ukraine and the message MAY YOUR SOUL REST IN ETERNAL PEACE AS YOU ENTER THE KINGDOM OF HEAVEN TO BE UNITED WITH YOUR PRINCE. A thistle pinned to a tree trunk and attached to a sheet of white card, upon it written the words:

'Your Majesty, Thank you from us All.' A badly drawn image of the Queen framed by a rainbow and flanked by a cheery pig and a cartoon character Mick could not identify, above the message 'Love from Hong Kong'. A child's drawing of the Queen sitting at a table facing Paddington Bear, the artist identifying herself as 5. Another child's drawing, showing a frowning emoji face shedding four tears, beneath the words 'The Queen died!' A family with a double-barrelled surname, below the message: 'Thank you for ruling with dignity and integrity; Elegance [*sic*] and class. We are honoured to have witnessed the longest reigning monarch.' Thanks from the Jackson family, with all six names given, as well as those of their dog, Tommy, and their snake, Elvis.

Mick left Green Park and plunged into Mayfair. At Shepherd Market he passed Jack the Clipper, which contained two barbers but no clients. He sauntered through the silence of the cigar shop neighbourhood. When he reached crowded Oxford Street he crossed it quickly and headed for Manchester Square. A new sign had gone up since his last visit: *Urinating on the street is illegal and can result in a £500 fine.*

He circled the private garden which occupied the centre of the square and walked up the steps to The Wallace Collection. Once inside he turned left. He traversed the gift shop and stepped into the darkness of the Richard III exhibition. It was a paltry affair, consisting of the famous nineteenth-century oil painting of the Princes in the Tower plus a suit of armour made for the movie *The Lost King*. That was it, apart from a handful of information boards. He went into the next gallery, glancing at various cabinets of weapons, then went upstairs. He scrutinised the Canalettos, the portraits of Napoleon, the hermaphrodite statuette. Then back down to the toilets, a facility no septuagenarian can afford to neglect for very long.

He left the Wallace and strolled to Selfridges to see how his newly published novel *Mick's Take* was doing.

Mick's Take was his lockdown novel, published in his seventy-fourth year. It was the story of a man's life, covering the post-War period right up to the Russian invasion of

Ukraine. It had received almost unanimous acclaim for its political acumen and as a daring work of autofiction – a dazzling mix of autobiography and invention. Its central character, Mick Kane, is born in 1948. Mick Kane's life has many parallels to that of Mick Owen. He gets a schoolgirl pregnant and marries her – Gemma Haley was obviously based on Gwynedd Hooley. The marriage crumbles and ends in divorce. At this point the life and the fiction start to diverge. Gemma has a crime novel published: *The Husband Who Vanished.* A simple plot with a twist or three. The female narrator bashes her husband over the head with a hammer, then chops up the corpse and eats it. A fortnight of pan-fried steak and oven chips! The book is acclaimed as both a brilliant crime story and a dazzling feminist satire. It quickly outsells that year's titles from P. D. James and Ruth Rendell. Gemma Haley begins a lucrative career as a top-selling crime writer.

Mick Kane, meanwhile, marries Daphne English (all too patently Dippy Scott). Daphne's father is a Labour Cabinet minister. Mick is elected in 1979 and becomes a brilliant backbench MP. A fierce critic of Brexit and a leading opponent of Jeremy Corbyn's leadership, Mick Kane loses his seat in 2019. Political journalists hail him as the best Prime Minister the country never had.

Amid the subservient reviews a rare dissident was Dilly MacDonald in *The Glaswegian*, who wrote: 'It's a masterpiece of dull writing that slides and slaloms and eventually rollercoasters into enviably consummated guff. It takes real talent to do that.' Plus there was yet another suggestion of plagiarism. A central episode in the novel involved Mick Kane rushing to Berlin on the night the Wall came down. 'Jansenist' in *Private Eye* wrote:

> Coincidence, or more? *Brandenburg* is a fine spy novel by Henry Porter, published in 2005. The novel is set mostly in East Germany in the months before *Die Wende* and the collapse of the Berlin Wall. On the night of the surprise opening of the border, the main protagonist is wandering

about in East Berlin, trying to find his lover. He is caught up in the confusion, blunders across the border with the throng and eventually takes refuge in Cafe Adler, close to Checkpoint Charlie, where he confronts, amongst other things, various aspects of his complicated family history. Sound familiar? Yes, there are strong elements of similarity with one of the key episodes in *Mick's Take*. Cafe Adler did exist, of course, though now it seems to be closed, and perhaps everyone gravitated there on the night the wall came down. Maybe Britain's most illustrious novelist has read *Brandenburg*, maybe he hasn't, but Ed Sheeran gets taken to court for a lot less.

Social media had its say – mostly ecstatic, sometimes not so. Carpers on Twitter compared the novel unfavourably to the fiction of Rachel Cusk. Others perceived a debt to Knausgård. One impudent fellow ('Lefty') detected clichés, muddled metaphors, flabby similes, pleonasms, catachresis, and numerous other sins against grammar and fine writing. But the critics and carpers were in every quarter obliterated by a tsunami of praise and adulation. Some fans cleverly spotted the allusion to Orson Welles's masterpiece embedded in the hero's surname. Those of greater critical acumen noted the tribute to one of Britain's greatest actors. In interviews Mick happily acknowledged that this was indeed his intention. 'Prufrock measured out his life in coffee spoons,' he told the young woman from *The Sunday Times*. 'Mine has been punctuated throughout by the films of Michael Caine.'

Not that he always knew it at the time. Caine had a barely visible bit part in *Carve Her Name with Pride* (1958), which had a shattering impact on Mick when he first saw it at the age of ten. The execution scene – so sudden, so unexpected, so squalidly miserable in its setting – haunted him still. Whereas at the time he scarcely remembered *The Day the Earth Caught Fire* (1961), a preposterous yarn based on the idea that the planet overheated to such an extent that all human life was threatened and society began to collapse. Even as a thirteen-year-old, Mick deplored fantasy, pessimism and wild exaggeration.

No, it wasn't until that bright Technicolour drama *Zulu* (1964) that the name Michael Caine first entered his consciousness. It was reinforced by *The Ipcress File* (1965), which brought out in Mick a fierce identification with the laconic Harry Palmer. He purchased the single of the soundtrack and played it repeatedly. He *was* Harry Palmer. Inspired by the film, Mick also bought his first coffee grinder. *The Ipcress File* imparted a wonderful truth about life: grinding beans impressed girls. After that it was a matter of hit after hit – *Alfie* (1966), *The Italian Job* (1969), *Battle of Britain* (1969). (Best to overlook *The Magus*.) And then came what was surely Caine's greatest film: *Get Carter* (1971). Mick never tired of viewing it.

For private reasons he had a particular affection for *The Romantic Englishwoman* (1975) – but he never spoke of it. Not to Sam Quiggly and not even to Delphine. And after that... Well, they were serviceable movies. *The Man Who Would Be King* (1975) – OK. *The Eagle Has Landed* (1976) – not awful. *A Bridge Too Far* (1977) – a fun film for boys. And then some rather barren years – it would be a kindness not to mention *Bullet to Beijing* (1995) and *Midnight in St Petersburg* (1996). Then a return to credibility with *Last Orders* (2001) – not that Mick particularly enjoyed it. Old men, on the whole, are not an interesting species. They fart with great frequency; they reminisce at inordinate length; they are always urgently needing the lavatory. For the elderly the melancholy present is perpetually grey and rainy, the joyous past a matter of blue skies and glorious sunlight.

Then *The Quiet American* (2002) – not great but not bad either. Ditto *Harry Brown* (2009). And then the Christopher Nolan films... Mick was not a fan of Nolan. His movies promised much but ended up being as nutritious as candy floss. All gimmick, no substance. *Inception* (2010); *Interstellar* (2014); the incomprehensible, tiresome and uninteresting *Tenet* (2020). (Mick had never liked jigsaw puzzles, not even when manufactured by James Joyce.) For that matter Mick didn't much like *Dunkirk* (2017) either. But a glorious return to form for MC with *Youth* (2015). At last! Perhaps old men weren't such narcissistic dullards after all...

4

Mick went to the back of the basement, where Selfridges had a disappointingly small book section. There an angry flush erupted on his leathery cheeks. *Mick's Take* was only number four in the Selfridges top ten! Unbelievable.

He glanced round. He was the only person in this part of the store. The nearest shoppers were in other sales areas, entranced by bright expensive goods. Selfridges was a little like the afterlife illustration in a Jehovah's Witness leaflet: a zone where light beamed down on plenitude and everyone seemed to be smiling.

In one quick grab Mick removed the volume at Number One, the autobiography of some black guy who edited *Vogue*. (It had received mixed reviews and been justifiably ridiculed in *Private Eye*. Apparently the author believed that Crufts was a dog race! It was extraordinary that no one at a major publishing house had spotted this howler, on the text's long journey to publication.)

He switched the books. Easy-peasy. Now *Mick's Take* was number one!

With a smile of contentment Mick went up the escalator to the ground floor and out the side entrance. He passed the spot where Sandra had died. That stretch of grey, slightly chipped kerb flanked by lemon stripes was his personal memento mori. It always made him shiver a little. Death can come utterly without warning. And Christ, what a dingy place to breathe your last – in an air-polluted side street off Oxford Street!

Mick emerged from his reverie and hailed a passing taxi. It is a reality rarely acknowledged that if you stand on a central London street between 8am and 4pm you are never sixty seconds from the approach of a black cab. They are even more ubiquitous than the capital's rats.

The cabbie dropped him off close to his second home, by a convenience store that sold newspapers. He went in and bought a copy of *The Times*. Back home at the mews he cracked open a Blue Moon lager and began to read about the deceased Dame.

Mantel dies working on new novel was the headline, above pictures of the Dame wearing a half-deflated bell tent and Sir Mark Rylance in a Tudor television costume. Mick's brow furrowed, his nose grew taut, his nostrils flared, his cheeks developed an angry flush as he read that she was 'acclaimed by many as the greatest British writer of her generation'.

Seventeen books to her name.

In 1990 elected as a Fellow of the Royal Society of Literature.[34]

Wolf Hall 'brought her international attention and her first Brooker [*sic*] Prize. *Bring Up the Bodies* won the prize three years later, 'making Mantel the first woman and the only Briton to win it twice'. Her place in *The Guinness Book of Records* assured. Immortal forever [*sic*].

34 'Fellow of the Royal Society of Literature': Royalty is, of course, in its cretinous philistinism – the mass murder of game birds, horse racing, foxhunting, militarism – the antithesis of anything remotely literary. The Royal Society of Literature comprises more than 600 Fellows, who are entitled to use the post-nominal letters FRSL. The existence of this preposterous organisation is a testament to the vanity and sycophancy of Britain's mediocre intelligentsia. New fellows of the Royal Society of Literature are elected by its current fellows. To be nominated for fellowship, a writer must have published two works of literary merit (a category determined by sales and the risible 'values' of corporate publishing). Nominations must be seconded by an RSL fellow. All nominations are presented to members of the Council of the Royal Society of Literature, who vote biannually to elect new fellows. The current rabble of literary titans includes Martin Amis, Anne Applebaum, Simon Armitage, David Baddiel, William Boyd, Tracy Chevalier, Jonathan Coe, Esther Freud, Timothy Garton Ash, Linda Grant, Roy Hattersley, Nick Hornby, Howard Jacobson, The Duke of Kent, Sir Andrew Motion, Sir Ferdinand Mount, Adam Nicolson (The Lord Carnock), The Hon. Gerard Noel, Ian Rankin, Frederic Raphael, J. K. Rowling, The Viscount Runciman of Doxford, Lady Stothard, Simon Windbag-Montefiore, Posy Simmonds, Polly Stenham, King Charles III and The Right Reverend the Lord Williams of Oystermouth.

'J. K. Rowling, the Harry Potter author, said: "We've lost a genius."'

The President of the Royal Society of Literature, Bernardine Evaristo, bubbled: 'We have been so lucky to have such a massive talent in our midst.' Mick smiled mirthlessly. *Massive* was certainly an apt adjective in two ways, he felt, finishing his lager and starting another.

Top literary critic Nicola Sturgeon commented that it was 'impossible to overstate the significance of the literary legacy Hilary Mantel leaves behind'.

Nicholas Pearson, her editor, said he had met her in Devon last month and she had talked excitedly about the new novel she'd started. 'That we won't have the pleasure of any more of her words is unbearable.' (Mick felt himself blessed; he could bear their absence with complete equanimity.)

Bill Hamilton of the Big Fish Agency gushed: 'Her wit, stylistic daring, creative ambition and phenomenal historical insight mark her out as one of the greatest novelists of our time.'

There was even a *Times* editorial, hailing her as a towering talent, a true twenty-first century literary great, a woman who had 'the respect of a mass audience' and who was also 'prolific, leaving behind a stellar legacy of novels, short stories and journalism'. She would, the thunderer thundered, 'continue to be read and admired for decades, if not centuries, to come'. Mick's scowl became scowlier.

Finally, he skipped through the long obituary. He was startled to learn that she had been 'a radical socialist' as a university student – a vague description which crystallized as membership of The Young Communist League. Mick did a quick Wikipedia check. This was 'The Youth Section of the Communist Party of Great Britain'. Odd. Mantel had gone in 1970 to the LSE to study Law but switched to Sheffield – when? – and graduated in 1973. As Mick knew, those were strange years to sign up to the CP. This was a time when radicals gravitated to the various fractions of contemporary British Trotskyism. The CP was old hat. It was discredited. *Neither*

Washington nor Moscow was the slogan of the cutting edge Left. So – there was a back story there but no one was narrating it. You'd have to wait for the biography. Presumably out there somewhere Mantel had her own Sam Quiggly, circling the fresh cold meat with hungry excited eyes.

Mick read on.

'Mantel would relax by watching cricket.' Jesus! That mind-numbing sport, every bit as tedious as darts or snooker. Not that Mick watched any sport. Not even football. Football was for people who required the stimulations of tribal identity and had something missing in their lives. People who enjoyed watching sport were like people who owned cats or dogs. They had a craving for slavish obedience which masked their private neediness.

Mantel had planned to move to Ireland, ostensibly as a protest against Brexit. But it was also a tax avoidance strategy, thanks to the agreeable Irish policy of exempting corporate publishing authors from taxation on their income.

The former radical socialist was made a Dame in 2014. How proud she must have been of the motto of her honour: 'For God and the Empire'.

Mick's scowlier scowl became its scowliest as he learned that Mantel was the only living author to have her picture on display in the National Portrait Gallery. He hadn't known that. Next his frown relaxed and morphed into a metallic chuckle as he read that Mantel's appearance was 'distinctive' in her 'capacious' dresses.

Quite.

And then The End.

Dame Hilary Mantel DBE FRSL, author, was born on July 6, 1952. She died of a stroke on September 2, 2022, aged 70.

He'd only just finished reading when Delphine arrived back from Paris. Kisses, hugs, a fuck. Then a bath together. Then towelling each other dry. Delphine kneeling. An attempted blowjob. But he stayed floppy. The ignition wouldn't start. Besides, he was out of juice.

That evening they went to their favourite private dining club in Westminster. A table was always available for their valued member Sir Owen. His presence added lustre to the dining experience of the other guests. No one ever asked him for an autograph – that would have been vulgarity incarnate.

The club had a gorgeous ambience of artfully arranged mirrors, discreet lighting, vases of fresh flowers. The tiled, dimly lit lavatories were exquisitely clean. They had napkins and bottled water.

Waiters, often from the ethnic community, dressed immaculately in black suits and elegant white shirts. Waitresses, also in black, wore short skirts. The manager, Albert, was always hovering, noting proceedings, anxious to satisfy the whims of every diner. Exquisite food, the finest wine. The roar of conversation; of happy, very wealthy people.

Afterwards Mick was in the mood to stroll home rather than take a cab. It was almost a mile but sometimes he felt the need to bring out his inner Charles Dickens and walk among the capital's poor.

On the deserted thoroughfares off Victoria Street the homeless were fashioning a room for the night in the capacious porches and entrances of commercial premises in which all the lights were off. Shadowy figures, often hooded, groped in Bags For Life for blankets, and stooped over misshapen bundles. This, Mick reflected, was one of the possible fates of all those poor wretches in society who had never managed to embrace the art of writing popular fiction.

Strangely, as you emerged into Westminster's brightly lit highways, where long-legged manikins in storefronts stared at luminous vistas of luxury goods, the dark iron inspection chamber covers underfoot leaked a distinct odour of faeces. The phenomenon was evident on not just one street but on all. The entire neighbourhood to the south and west of Buckingham Palace was laced with an unavoidable stench.

'We should 'ave taken a taxi,' Delphine grumbled, wrinkling her nose.

Next day Mick went north to Kipling Manor to work on his new novel and Delphine returned to France. Her father had, quite unexpectedly, been taken ill. It sounded serious. She hoped it would not turn out simply to be a plot device to ensure that she was separated from her husband at a time of sudden, urgent need.

5

Mick, refreshed by his London trip, sits once more at his desk in his tower room. On the wall, in elegant grey frames, are some of his more recent reviews.

2021. *The Obscurer* review section.

Mick Owen's Books of the Year

- △ David Baddiel's *Jews Don't Count* is a chilling but necessary book about people who have criticised him on Twitter. As David says, in Berlin in 1934 the Gestapo would have come looking for him. This is something Jeremy Corbyn never mentioned once in any of his speeches. Shameful.
- △ Amanda Smyth's *Fortune* is a mesmerising tale of desire and ambition set against the background of the oil industry in Trinidad in the 1920s. The lavish technical details of oil drilling are as astonishing as the fast-paced plot and the lush evocative prose. The climax quite literally stunned me.
- △ Too many people think that 'trans' is the plural of 'small portable radio'. After Torrey Peters' *Detransition, Baby* no one will ever make that mistake again! This is the dazzling tale of three typical New Yorkers: Reese, a trans woman who dated Ames when she was Amy, and Katrina, who became pregnant from Ames, who has detransitioned. A vibrant, thoughtful, essential book about everyday life and parenting, which truly captures the zeitgeist.

Mick writes fast, consumed by inspiration. He's at the top of his game. In full flow. He reflects that it must have been just like this for Shakespeare, hunched over a sheet of parchment at midnight in that house on Silver Street. The flicker of candlelight. The quill zig-zagging across the empty space like a jigging, restless heart monitor. Inky fingers, just like those of Joseph Fiennes in that marvellous, wonderful, brilliantly convincing representation, *Shakespeare in Love*.

The thought made Mick wonder what had happened to Joseph Alberic Twisleton-Wykeham-Fiennes. He couldn't recall seeing him in any movie since. A quick dip into Wikipedia supplied the answer. Alberic wasn't by a long chalk a failure. He was plainly making serious money (good man!) and his services were still in demand. But alas, all those titles in the inventory of his later film career were turkeys, flops, fizzlers. He'd not had a serious hit since the time of Shakespeare.

Such was life. Some went on to greatness; others entered a period of slow decline. Mick couldn't help remembering his old mate Clive Sinclair. He was dead, now, poor chap. No danger now of his ever making a comeback and producing a late, wholly unexpected masterpiece. He owed it to Clive for helping him deal with those wearisome types who'd objected to his trip to Israel to collect The Tel Aviv Freedom Medal. The medal was given annually to a writer selected for 'Outstanding bravery in standing firm against totalitarianism, terror and tyranny'. There had been a letter in *The Guardian* urging Mick not to go, signed by people he had barely heard of. There was that wearisome film director who did all those dreary socialist realist kitchen sink dramas. There was the ambient music man. There was the fantasy writer China Miéville. One glance at his photograph indicated (bald man with giant earrings) that he was gay. One had nothing against homosexuals, of course. But they all too often had angry bees buzzing around in their bright pink bonnets. Besides, fantasy was not Mick's cup of tea – wizards and dragons and brave little Hobbits. Infantile.

So he had gone, made his speech, suggested that the settlement programme be slowed down so that negotiations could take place. He had been photographed shaking hands with Amos Oz, a marvellous man and writer. And at the end of his speech he had produced his sensational initiative (it was Amos who had actually suggested it and done a lot of the spadework). Mick solemnly announced that he was delighted to become the Patron of an entirely new project, which would bring the two sides together and further the cause of peace. *The Jerusalem Wind Orchestra*. Mick had been happy to pay for the trumpets.

The Orchestra involved twelve Israeli Jews, three Palestinians from the Gaza Strip, three Palestinians from the West Bank, and six Palestinians from Jerusalem. The Orchestra had been a considerable success in its first year, attracting grants from a variety of international organisations. The BBC made an hour-long documentary about it, featuring interviews with Amos and Mick. After a year one heard less of the Orchestra and two years later it disbanded, after all the Palestinian members had met unfortunate ends. The three from Gaza had died when their school was bombed in an Israeli raid during Operation Cockroach Removal. The three from the West Bank had been shot dead during an undercover security operation, and it was surely not the fault of the IDF snipers that they had mistaken the trumpets for weapons. Of the Jerusalem musicians, four had been shot dead in their car on their way to rehearsals – once again an innocent mistake by security personnel who believed that the instruments were rifles – and the other two were crushed to death in their homes when they were bulldozed to make way for the expansion of a settlement.

It was all very sad. Mick felt he had done his best for peace in the Middle East. Fortunately the deaths of the twelve Palestinian musicians were not reported by the BBC or any of the other corporate media, so it was commonly believed that the orchestra was still out there somewhere, playing agreeable versions of classics by Tchaikovsky, Dvořák and other greats. It later turned out that five of the Jewish members of the orchestra had been directly involved in the killing of the Palestinian musicians, but this revelation only appeared on an obscure web page run by an independent news organisation.

This was subsequently shut down by the server after an organisation which devoted itself to spotting anti-Semitism realised that this report about the orchestra caused hurt and alarm to members of the Jewish community.

Yes, poor old Clive Sinclair. A trajectory from minor commercial success to declining sales, death and critical oblivion. It probably didn't help that people confused him with a famous inventor. Whereas with Mick it was the reverse. Success led to greater success. Greater success led to global success. He was now a superstar. In the early days of search engines when he typed in 'Mick' his surname was way down the list. Then, eventually, he was nudging the top three. In time he dislodged Fleetwood. Hucknall also experienced slippage. At last Mick was breathing down the wrinkled neck of the legendary Stone.

Mick had always been amused by the down to earth woman from Bedford who, upon meeting Jumping Jack Flash face to face, later confided: 'I wanted to give him a good iron.' And now, finally, the lizard-skinned jitterbugger had been displaced. When you typed the word 'Mick' into Google or any other search engine what jumped up next was not 'Jagger' but 'Owen'. The novelist was home and dry. He was the winner. He was like Picasso or the early Beatles. Now even a hastily scrawled shopping list was a relic of inestimable worth.

Scribble, scribble, scribble.

Tap, tap, tap.

Light at the End of the Tunnel will tell the tale of a brilliant heart surgeon trapped in the Limehouse Link by environmental protesters who have glued themselves to the tarmac at the exit. The surgeon – Ron? Ben? – something monosyllabic – is racing to hospital to save the life of a child badly injured in a road accident. Ben (possibly Ron) runs to the tunnel exit in a vain attempt to reason with the protesters. Only the arrival of the SAS, who dig up the road and rush the surgeon to the crash scene by jet-pack, saves the day.

Mick writes in longhand, very fast, pouring out his ideas for the plot, the characters, the back stories (a faithful labrador, a

Corbynista who paints anti-Semitic messages on the wall of his local synagogue, a malicious lesbian, a degenerate dentist). Later he types it up. He feels a familiar thrill.

Indubitably, another masterpiece is being born.

6

Sam Quiggly sat at an open window, knocking back his last Jim Beam of the night.

The jewelled city twinkled far below.

In the curvaceous buttock of darkness that was the Bay a few pinpricks of scarlet light wavered gently like the target markers of an advanced laser weapon fixing their position.

It was 2am and he felt very tired and a little despondent. It was another of those nights when he regretted ever getting involved with a biography of Mick Owen. Once it had made him feel massively important. He had been chosen as the conduit of genius. He was the accountant of a human life gifted with a facility for words enjoyed by few others: Updike, unquestionably; Roth, obviously; Joyce, perhaps – though the jury was still out there. And one hardly needed to mention the author of *The History of Cardenio*.

Back then he had felt immensely privileged by his annual trips to see Mick. They dined together. Mick supplied the contours of his past. He was charming, helpful, and enthusiastic about the biography. When the waitress arrived with the bill Mick, gratifyingly, always snatched it up at once and absolutely insisted on paying. He said it was the least he could do for the man who would reinforce his reputation for eternity. Sam repaid his benefactor with ecstatic reviews of each new title in the pages of *Atlantic Monthly*, *Entertainment Weekly*, *The New Yorker*, *Salon*, *The San Francisco Chronicle*, *Time*, *The Wall Street Journal* and *The Washington Post*. Mick's new one, he let readers know, was every bit as good as his last one. Dazzling, resplendent, graceful, magisterial, glorious, astonishing, humane, enthralling, extraordinary, ambitious, acute, absorbing, seductive, compassionate, gorgeous, bewitching, thoughtful, provocative, marvellous, beautiful, wrenching, ingenious, expansive, memorable, suspenseful, extraordinary, magical, bracing, powerful, shattering, sublime, transformative, riveting, convincing, vivid, disturbing, elegant, precise, luminous. Sam's old wrinkled dictionary had a sore bottom from overwork.

But now the years had rolled by and his Owen biography had become bloated. It had grown fatter and fatter and fatter. Now the text was much like one of those vast, rippling women with hippo bellies and elephant-size asses you frequently encountered obstructing an aisle in Wal-Mart. It was years ago that the manuscript had gotten longer than J. Michael Lennon's *Norman Mailer*. His publishers had become nervous. Apart from the attention-span issue – as prevalent in Great Britain as west of Quoddy Head – most Americans have fairly weak arms. They don't like books they can't pick up.

Sam suggested splitting the book into two volumes, like Boyd's Nabokov bio. His prestigious publishers, Aimless House, were enthusiastic. Two vols meant double sales! But he had left Brian Boyd's anorexic volumes far behind. Now Sam Quiggly had even overtaken Norman Sherry and his three-volume take on Graham Greene. The fact was there was so much more to say about Mick Owen than a minor writer like Greene. He needed four volumes to say what needed to be said. Perhaps, all things considered, a fifth. Six at the most, he was pretty certain. No – make that seven. His agent, Shell Hoover, though breezy, bright and as dog-puddle-shallow as literary agents commonly are, was quietly appalled. The symptoms of lymphogranuloma venereum are commonly found among writers. Commercial success all too frequently results in elephantiasis (Rowling; le Carré). But Sam was not yet a star – merely an incoming meteorite of uncertain luminosity. Shell urged him to keep shtum. Once Owen was dead they could discuss cuts. In the meantime she left Quiggly to his own devices (a defused grenade from a Normandy beach; a yellow one-man submarine raised from the bed of Loch Hell; a longcase clock autographed by Laurence Sterne; a marine chronometer, once the property of Rupert Gould).

Yawning, Sam Quiggly peeled off his crumpled blue Great Gatsby T-shirt and his stained 501s. He attended to his bladder and his teeth, then crawled into bed. As he slept, a small dime-sized stain appeared at the crotch of his chequered boxer shorts. Before long it had spread to become a dollar. During his dreaming more coins would appear.

7

In Paris Delphine spent a fortnight in the 5th Arrondissement attending to her poor father's morphine-swamped end. He babbled of blue fields, red flags and striped windmills.

Mick had not accompanied her, knowing all too well that Ferdinand Diderot detested him for his politics and his conventional narrative forms. Diderot had visited Kipling Manor just once. He insisted it must have been built from the proceeds of slavery. Mick was able to refute this but Diderot contradicted him. The historical record had patently been falsified. He advised Mick to dig a little deeper. Mick sighed and went to bed.

Ferdinand was, Mick felt, just another disappointed *soixante-huitard*. He maintained an enduring commitment to the politics of Marx and Lenin. His favourite movies were *The Battle of Algiers* and *La Chinoise*. In fiction his highest regard was for Marguerite Duras, post-*Moderato cantabile*. He clung to narratives which had long since lost their marketability. He maintained his handle on an outmoded politics. The sensible members of both Ferdinand's and Mick's generations had long ago transferred their grip from Marcuse paperbacks to Le Creuset casserole dishes, cast iron saucepans and all the paraphernalia of a well-equipped kitchen. Cooking was the new politics. In this, Mick was ahead of his time. He had long ago withdrawn interest in Parliamentary matters and economic crises and wars, shutting himself away with that seminal text, *Mastering The Art of French Cooking*, well before the era of celebrity chefs and nightly TV shows.

Poor Ferdinand. Sam Quiggly had tried to talk to him but every overture was rebuffed. Now the troubled Frenchman was dying. He had always been Mick's most unrelenting critic. His father-in-law informed him that *Restitution* was nothing more than the accomplished simulacrum of an Edwardian novel – a shiny and synthetic text focused on affluent liberal lifestyles and designed to flatter the values of a decaying European bourgeoisie, which sought the comforts of nostalgia and the easy-going, unchallenging entertainment that went by the name of 'literary fiction'. Ferdinand also noted that on the fringes of Mick's plots were Leftists and radicals, who were invariably represented as dull-witted, obtuse, hypocritical, totalitarian in spirit, wholly fatuous. Occasionally they were also creepy sex predators. He wondered if one or two of them were not in fact intended as sly satires upon himself.

And now Ferdinand was dying.

And then he was dead.

Delphine flew into Stansted. She'd arranged that Mick would go back with her to Paris for the interment at Père Lachaise. In the meantime she'd left others to organise the funeral. Perhaps at this late stage a brother could be born, fully formed and of mature years. Her brother could sort out all the tedious formalities which are required after a death. A brother – a half-brother it would need to be – could easily be arranged, narratologically speaking. Long before marrying Ferdinand, Delphine's mother, as a teenager, had given birth to a secret love child. Pierre. Adoption. Brother and sister not reunited for decades. A delightful and moving back story. In the land of Annie Ernaux this was more than likely.

Once through arrivals Delphine hired a BMW and headed for the A12 and home. Along the first section of the fast road to Braintree the sun was an orange orb on a bed of blue velvet cloud. By the time she reached the highway to Ipswich it was night. Her dipped lights slashed the star-spangled sky as she passed over the Orwell Bridge. The traffic slackened off after the Woodbridge turn, and slackened off some more when she passed the sign to Aldeburgh. Patricia Highsmith had once lived in that town, in a narrow three-storey house on the pebbled seafront, not far from that quaint feature, the Lookout Tower. Highsmith was there in November 1963, when Kennedy was shot.

Yoxford was as empty as it always was after dark. A curl of yellow moon hung over the village like a magical cheese. Delphine could almost smell its rich tangy aroma. *Cheesy*, she thought. Her mind filled with the image of their blade-indented wooden board, deliciously arranged with Bleu d'Auvergne, Brie de Meaux, Camembert, Roquefort, blue-veined Stilton... A cheesy ending to a meal is a flavoursome and tasty one. The same applies to novels that sell. Mick had learned from Sandra Locke that simple golden truth.

Delphine followed the road westward, passing the sign SCENIC ROUTE. Soon afterwards she turned off, following familiar narrow rural roads along the twisting route to Kipling Manor. But as she motored along that final stretch of hedgerow-crowded track she became aware of a strange glow in the sky. Was it dawn already? *Pas possible!*

Her eyes narrowed as she drew closer to her destination. When all this was over she would need to visit her optician.

The tops of the trees were tinted with scarlet paint. A flurry of grey snow coated the windshield. She flicked on the wipers.

At the brushed-steel entry machine by the gated entrance she punched in the required four numbers. The barrier slid aside. She passed between the stone pineapples – in so much better state than first seen all those years ago – and accelerated through a blizzard down the crimson drive.

Mon Dieu!

An inferno greeted her bulging, astonished, appalled eyes.

The entire house was ablaze. Fire dripped from the windows and slipped down the brickwork like some luminous yellow fluid vomited by a giant.

Even as she slammed on the brakes and skidded to a halt she felt the heat. It rushed at her, like a surge of hot dry air from a tent at the Hay-on-Wye Festival. The interior of the BMW began to boil, like a kettle. She quickly engaged reverse and retreated forty metres.

Delphine sprang out and stared as if bewitched. She watched as the double bed from their room came tumbling down, trailing sparks and wriggling tongues of flame. It was followed by the second-best bed, which they saved for visiting Shakespeare scholars.

Beams began to collapse. One wing simply vanished in a puff of smoke. She screamed: '*Mick!*'

Where in hell was he?

In hell, that's where.

Suddenly she saw him. The lights in the house had long since been extinguished by the melting of the electrical wiring. Now fire lit up like daylight the tower. As she watched she saw the window frame on her side fall away and crash into the heart of the burning house. Beyond it, brilliantly illuminated by fire, was Mick.

He was not alone.

There was a woman with him.

They were embracing, as lovers do. Delphine's pulse thudded like a drum in a Haitian voodoo ceremony. Trembling, she felt a spasm of jealous rage. She shuddered. She had been absent and during that time he'd had a woman in the house, in their bed. The horror, the horror... Suddenly Delphine realised who this woman was. *Mon Dieu!* It was Gillian Logan. Her cropped red hair and strange frog-like face were unmistakeable.

It was astonishing; unbelievable. Mick hadn't mentioned this abominable woman for years. They'd both assumed she'd died ages ago – a slow, final descent into total obscurity. No one read Gillian Logan any more. If she was remembered at all it was only in connection with Mick and her ancient, nonsensical claims of plagiarism. Logan's last novel was published back in 1999. None since. *House of Shadows*. The story of Justin Lancing, a reclusive author who in his younger days had his heart broken forever. Justin had written the draft of a dazzling first novel, *The Last Train to Waverley*, about a passionate romance in Edinburgh with an older married woman. But she had stolen his only copy of the manuscript and given it to her husband. It was her peace offering as she returned to the brute and cruelly dumped Justin. She'd expected Derek, her husband, to destroy the manuscript. Instead he'd made a few changes, then published it under his own name. It was a massive success. Justin Lancing's putative literary career fizzled out and he became a supply teacher. In old age he lived alone, in penury, which was not far from Leith.

Was that last book autobiographical? In Gillian Logan's life there had been the faint hint of an affair. She had once enjoyed, briefly, a 'close friendship' with Jacques Derrida. Was this Sonia Orwell and Merleau-Ponty all over again?

Years ago Sam Quiggly had tried to interview Gillian but he had been rebuffed. His biography would nevertheless require a carefully worded acknowledgement of her 1981 novel *Theft and Loss*. It contained, after all, the first representation in fiction of Mick Owen as a 'character'.

Theft and Loss is a bleak tale about a woman who writes an extraordinary first novel drawn from her experiences as an abused adolescent who then leaves home and enters into a destructive relationship with a manipulative older man. Plainly autobiographical but coolly detached and stylish, it's entitled *Concrete Facts*. An agent expresses great interest in the manuscript, which the heroine transports personally to the agent's London office. But on the underground, getting off at Oxford Circus, she mistakenly picks up the wrong carrier bag. As she stands on the platform and glances inside she sees to her horror that it contains not her manuscript but the fifth volume of a 1957 children's encyclopaedia. Despite her best efforts the lost manuscript, her only copy, is never recovered.

Broken by this loss the heroine never attempts to write again. Years pass and her life becomes a spiral of drugs, drink, abortions, and a series of destructive relationships with unsuitable men. At the age of sixty she buys a copy of *Concrete Realities*, an acclaimed first novel by Mark Ewing, a young writer hailed as an extraordinary talent. Reading it, she is stunned to discover it is her old manuscript, word for word, with only the title changed. The heroine obtains a revolver and sets off to assassinate Ewing, who is due to give a reading at the London Review of Books bookshop in Bloomsbury. When she finally encounters Ewing in the flesh she perceives 'a pale, weedy individual with longish hair parted down the middle, John Lennon glasses, lobeless ears and tight, thin lips. The eyes were slits of calculation, the smile slightly crooked. He looked like a malnourished hawk searching for something dead and easily edible.'

The heroine produces her weapon and a deadly hush falls upon the audience. Ewing's complexion turns to ash. But at the last moment, instead of killing Ewing, she screams 'Thief! Impostor!' – and turns the gun on herself. The End.

The publication of *Theft and Loss* passed almost without notice. The only high-profile review was in *The Spectator*, by A. N. Wilson. He gave it extravagant praise, acclaimed it as a minor masterpiece, and added waspishly, 'We all know who Mark Ewing really is!'

Mick's agent made him aware of this narrative development but advised him to say nothing. Sound advice. Logan's work attracted only indifference, except in France, where all her books were translated and she was regarded as an important writer. But that's Europe for you. They have strange tastes in the novel, alien to the sturdy English realist tradition of middle-class professionals suffering First World problems in agreeable domestic and rural settings.

Gillian Logan had become reclusive, deeply private. Was she another Rosemary Tonks? Lots of sleeping around in her younger days, followed by religious obsession and a burning sense of sin and horror at the ubiquitous human depravity around her? Was that it? The rest of her life devoted to decades of self-disgust, Biblical furies, and dusty sexless solitude? Or was it not that at all? Was she simply a lesbian who preferred not to flaunt it? Or had she never had carnal knowledge of another? Was she, in fact, merely a wrinkled celibate? Or, better (far better from a biographer's POV), its opposite: a nymphomaniac of prodigious and extreme appetites who attended masked orgies and popped out every weekend to the woods for a spot of dogging? Another person's sex life is always a mystery but hers was as murky and opaque as they – so to speak – come.

Delphine realised that she was mistaken. They were not locked together in passion but fighting. It was a wrestling match. Gillian Logan was clawing at his face, drawing blood. Her bent fingers were trying to rake his eyes. Mick bobbed his head back, desperately trying to push her away. His white shirt was bright with blood. He had been repeatedly knifed. It was amazing he could stand at all.

How old was Gillian Logan now? Delphine was uncertain but knew she must be at the very least in her eighties. For an octogenarian she seemed remarkably sprightly. No matter how he writhed, Mick couldn't shake her off. So! *Zut alors!* This demented woman had come after all this time for her revenge. She was currently in the process of obtaining it.

Later, the forensic experts would work out what had occurred. Gillian (quite obviously inspired by the climax of that marvellous movie, *The Killer Inside Me*) had moved from floor to floor, splashing petrol on carpets, curtains, sofas, easy chairs, difficult chairs, bookshelves – everything. Meanwhile Mick, upstairs in his study, concentrating on his laptop screen, Chopin tinkling gently in the background, was blissfully unaware of the inferno which was being prepared beneath him. It seemed he had been so deep in his work-in-progress that he knew nothing of his adversary's presence in his house. Her arrival had been recorded from multiple angles – but no one was watching the CCTV monitors. Mick had not heard the breaking of glass in the downstairs lounge window. Because he was expecting Delphine to return soon all the alarm systems had been switched off.

It was only when Gillian wrenched open the door and entered, a knife clenched in each fist, that the reality hit him. She arrived in the room attended around her shoulders by surges of crisp fresh smoke. It made her seem like an emissary of Satan.

Across the floors beneath the antagonists a continuous crackling could be heard (especially by the resident mice), punctuated by small explosions and then louder bangs. The two novelists were last seen locked in a final embrace. Their clothes blazed, their hair was on fire. They seemed to scream in chorus – a terrible, unending scream which reminded Delphine of that now distant day when her lilo doze had been savagely interrupted by the dreadful news about Ishiguro's prize.

And then the floorboards gave way. The two novelists dropped as one into the centre of the inferno.

The screaming stopped

Now there was only the roar of a single pillar of fire and a loud ticking which seemed like the fierce, terrible measure of eternity.

8

Sam Quiggly woke.

It was dawn and a smoky haze filled his bedroom. *What the fuck?* He'd been having a strange dream about Delphine Owen. She'd driven home at night and found Kipling Manor ablaze. Gillian Logan had set it on fire and then killed Mick and herself. *Weird shit.*

Sam's dreams had been especially lurid lately. Repeatedly he'd learned from Twitter that Mick Owen was dead. The news went viral. Not since David Bowie had such a death touched the entire planet. And then he'd woken and there he was, Mick Owen, on the radio, genial, articulate, still very much alive. The dream had been classic Freudian wish-fulfilment.

Sam Quiggly climbed out of bed, coughing. His boxers released a distinct odour of urine. *Fuck it.* He was out of incontinence pads. Back to Wal-Mart...

Oh. My. God. Profoundly shaken, he barely croaked the three monosyllabic words.

The forest above his house was a wall of fire. Flames three storeys high were pressing down the slope towards him. The intense heat had cracked the windows of his Hyundai Palisade. Even as he watched the hood buckled. The car seemed to be fucking *melting*. And then it exploded. And then the windows of his house began to pop, one by one, like a sniper was shooting them out. And then somehow the wooden panels of his house were starting to smoulder.

Holy shit.

He saw that his neighbour's house down the hill was ablaze.

Sam dragged on jeans, a T-shirt, a pair of trainers and ran. He exited his house. The heat was unbelievable. It pressed against him like a plastic sheet.

He started to run down the dirt track. Smoke and flames seemed to be everywhere. His whole world was on fire. He tasted the smoke in his mouth, dirty and acrid. His throat started to hurt. His eyes brimmed with tears. His lungs felt weirdly hot and prickly, like someone had basted the linings with chilli pepper.

A random tongue of fire licked him and then retracted. He felt a searing pain. He became aware of his own skin hanging off him like rags. Wet white papery rags. He didn't know how he made it through that inferno. Maybe he was a character in a novel and he was not yet disposable. The author needed him for something.

In the thick boiling white smoke ahead of him a helmeted figure appeared. An astronaut? Sam felt faint. He started to topple.

The fireman caught him. He dragged Sam back.

Above the biographer the smoke boiled and shaped itself into wild, swirling patterns. Next, paramedics loomed out of the acrid smog. They lifted him on to a stretcher. As they were about to put him into an ambulance Sam saw above him the smoke take on the distinct outlines of Mick Owen's face, monstrously enlarged. It was him, no question – those narrowed eyes, the receding hair above the big forehead, the scholar's spectacles... The novelist's puffy grey lips seemed to break into a gigantic smile.

Then Sam was rolled inside the vehicle. The doors slammed shut.

It was only on the way to the hospital that Sam Quiggly realised he needed to go back. 'My book!' he screamed. It was all back at the house: the entire draft on his laptop, plus a back-up copy on a portable hard drive, plus more copies on memory sticks! He never left the house without taking at least two back-up copies with him.

When the medics told him they would not be going back he sat up and tried to break free. One of the medics pinioned his arms. The other one slid a needle in.

Sam fell back, unconscious.

Two days later his agent came to the hospital to see him.

'You've lost *everything*?' she said. She was incredulous. 'You didn't keep a *fucking back-up* in a *safe deposit box* or even with your *fucking sister*?'

No, he had not.

'Jesus.'

'But I've had an idea. Why don't I just distil all my research and recycle it as a novel?

'Bad idea.'

'*Good* idea, Shell.'

'Don't fuck with me, brother. I know this racket better than anyone. You know jack shit. Believe me when I say *it's a very bad idea.*'

'Maybe I need a new agent.'

'Maybe you do, sonny boy.' She stood. 'Goodbye, Sam. Call me if you ever revive your smoky biography. But don't call me up about no novel.'

'Goodbye, Shell.'

Like that Irish joker once wrote: *Goodbye, goodbye, goodbye*. Tomorrow, folks, is another day.

SQ
San Francisco
2022

Postscript

The story you have just read was forwarded to me as an unpublished manuscript by Sam Quiggly's attorney. He informed me that his late client had given me the rights to it, with publication entirely at my discretion. Sam also invited me to edit, amend or to add to or annotate the text as I saw fit.

Reading his narrative, I confess I was frequently startled. The assertion that Sam Quiggly had never met me was utterly false. The revelation that I had died was unexpected. When the reader last hears of me I am due to be interred at Père Lachaise. I must insist that I am, at the time of writing, very much alive. Moreover, I am not yet decrepit and doomed. As the English would say (in their usual charmingly meaningless fashion), I am 'all there with my cough drops'. And although I have no objection to a long, clammy stay at Père Lachaise, I must emphasize that – *hélas*! – no space has yet been reserved for me.

The description of what was purportedly my only stay at Kipling Manor is a travesty. I have allowed it to remain an example of the absurdity of biography. As a genre it is seamed with exaggeration, complete fantasy and important suppressed facts.

I should explain that Sam and I met several times. We got to know each other quite well. When Sam invited me to amend his text I believe he knew very well what he was doing, and which direction any interpolations of my own would take. I like to think his invitation had a mischievous dimension and I have acted accordingly.

The book you have just read is then, in the end, a joint production – literally so in the case of Sam, who, in my experience, rarely got through the day without smoking at least one large spliff. (My personal drugs, I should perhaps make clear, are merely those banal bourgeois addictions, coffee and wine – nothing more.)

In my son-in-law's rambling and badly written family saga *Mick's Take* there briefly appears the figure of François Mangeot. A sufferer from advanced scoliosis, Mangeot is a failed, embittered poet reduced to scratching a living as a waiter in a shabby backstreet café in the Latin Quarter. Of progressive views, Mangeot is shown to be a monster of Ted Hughesian proportions – a narcissist with perverted sexual tastes which have forced two wives down into tragically early graves. The reader is coolly told that this grotesque Frenchman is 'as twisted and malicious as Richard III, who also had two deaths on his conscience – except that neither man was in possession of such a sensitive mental accessory'. Mangeot is plainly, much of the time, a Haitian doll intended to be fashioned in my own image. Fortunately my dispassionate commitment to veracity has ensured that my shaping of Sam's fine narrative has prevented me from tampering in any way with his picture of a man widely acclaimed as a literary giant.

Quite what other changes and additions a *soixante-huitard* could possibly have made to *Concrete Impressions* is a matter I shall leave entirely to the reader to deduce.

Ferdinand Diderot
Rue du Coq d'Or
5th Arrondissement
Paris
2023

www.ingramcontent.com/pod-product-compliance
Lightning Source LLC
LaVergne TN
LVHW090954080826
845145LV00003B/1008

* 9 7 8 1 8 3 8 4 8 9 8 9 2 *